DATE DUE

BOOKS BY BRIAN W. ALDISS

Seasons in Flight

Seasons in Flight
BRIAN ALDISS

ATHENEUM   NEW YORK   1986

Some of these stories have appeared elsewhere: 'The Other Side of the Lake' in *Fiction Magazine* (1984); 'The Gods in Flight' in *Interzone* (1984); 'The Blue Background' in *Isaac Asimov's Science Fiction Magazine* (1983); 'Igur and the Mountain' in *A Christmas Feast* (Macmillan, 1983); 'The Girl Who Sang' in *Lands of Never*, edited by Maxim Jakubowski (Allen & Unwin, 1982); 'The Plain, the Endless Plain' in *Minnesota Review* (1984), 'The O in José' in *Impulse* (1966); and 'A Romance of the Equator' in the *Standard* (1979).

Library of Congress Cataloging in Publication Data

Aldiss, Brian Wilson, _____
   Seasons in flight.

   I. Title.   SCI FIC
PR6051.L3S4   1985   823'.914   84-24329
ISBN 0-689-11538-5

With love to Betty and Antony –
for Norfolk reading

Contents

Seasons in Flight

The Other Side of the Lake

The two villages faced each other across the arm of the lake. One was a poor village, and in decline, whereas the other was prosperous, and busy developing contacts with the outside world.

The villages differed in both nationality and religion, for the frontier between them ran down the middle of the lake. Although no more than four miles and a half of water separated them, God was worshipped in one village – when he was worshipped at all – in a building with a dome and a minaret, whereas, in the other village, he was worshipped in a square building with no minaret.

Even the climate differed from one village to the other. The poor village suffered from a chill wind which blew from the north and blighted its crops. The mountains which rose behind it curtailed its hours of sunlight; the peaks, on which snow could be seen even in early summer, cut off the warm evening sun from the village and its fields.

These mountains could be seen across the lake from the more prosperous village. But they formed merely a grand spectacle. The climate here was mild, its extremes moderated to some extent by the waters of the lake.

11

The lake was full of fish. The trout in particular were fine, and it was told in the more prosperous village how, in days gone by, trout were tickled from the lake, wrapped in vine-leaves, and carried alive by runners to grace the imperial tables in far Byzantium.

The poorer village had no such legends; few villagers cared to fish in the lake, because of dangerous currents close to the bank. However, there was one young man who fished regularly in the waters. He used to net large green frogs and beautiful trout, which he sold to or bartered with the other villagers.

This young fisherman's parents had died young, and he lived on his own in a tumbledown stone house of two rooms. The little house stood by the water's edge on the more infertile end of the village. From inside it, the slap-slap of the water against the stone jetty could always be heard. At evening, when he had got rid of his catch, the young fisherman would stand on the jetty and gaze across the lake at the other village, still bathed in sunlight.

One morning early, he climbed into his boat and, instead of fishing, rowed all the way across the lake.

To his right, the lake narrowed and was lost among trees. Beyond the trees, it widened again. There it became the possession of a third nation, a nation with access to a warm southern sea, a nation where − so it was rumoured − nobody worked much and the women were extremely beautiful and expert with the oily dishes of the south.

But the young fisherman kept his eyes on the east bank of the lake ahead, and did not look to either side.

A priest lived in the more prosperous village. He was a devout young man whose calling required him to remain celibate. However, a silent orphan girl of remarkable beauty came daily to clean his house, and her he loved deeply. On this day, the girl was not to be seen; she did not appear as usual at seven in the morning at the priest's house, and sent no word during the day. The priest went about his business with a rather absent mind.

In the evening, the young fisherman entered the priest's door and stood in his parlour clutching his leather hat in both hands. The fisherman's complexion was ruddy and robust from his outdoor life. The priest's complexion was pallid from a life spent under roofs; only his knees were red under his cassock, from hours of prayer. His curly black beard made his face look even more pale.

'I have come to ask your permission to court your servant girl, Grana,' said the fisherman.

The priest did not wish to say yes to this request because of his own interest in the girl. On the other hand, he did not want to say no, being afraid that people would then become suspicious of his motives.

On asking the fisherman a few questions, he discovered that he came from the village across the lake. The fisherman said that the first person he had seen when he arrived in the early morning and was tying up his boat was the servant girl, buying herself a bread roll on the quayside before starting her day's work. He had immediately fallen in love with her. He spoke to her. They had spent the day walking by the lake or in the fields which, at that time of year, were surrounded by hedgerows full of flowers and nesting birds. All this the young fisherman told the priest very simply and directly.

The priest listened with a gloomy face and downcast eyes. He asked finally, 'Does Grana return your feelings?'

'That you must ask Grana, sir.'

So the priest reluctantly gave his consent to the courtship. Thereafter, his servant girl came to his house punctually each morning and worked hard all day. Once, the priest seized her angrily and asked her what she was thinking about, but she pulled away from him and cursed him in no uncertain terms.

Then the priest became more careful, and remained silent and watchful, as was his nature. He persuaded a lad he knew to observe the servant in the evenings, and discovered that the fisherman, when the moon was full, was in the habit of rowing across the lake from the poorer village and meeting the servant girl, who waited for him on the silent quay. She would climb into his boat, whereupon it would move over the surface of the lake, to disappear into silence and the luminous dark. The priest crept down one night and saw it for himself.

It was two years before the young fisherman called at the priest's house again. He stood in the parlour, his head slightly bent because of the low ceiling, holding his hat in his hands. He said firmly that he wished to be married to the priest's servant girl.

The priest's sallow face went very pale. He said in a low voice, 'And does Grana wish to marry you?'

At which point in the conversation, the girl herself appeared, ran to the fisherman, and said, saucily, 'Why, I'm mad to marry him, and can't think of nothing else.'

So the priest gave his consent, fearing that if he did not, his parishioners would become suspicious of his motives.

Whereupon the fisherman said, 'And we want you to marry us, if you please.'

'There is a different religion where you come from, man.'

'I have no religion. She's the one with the religious feelings, so it is suitable that you should marry her to me.'

'Very well.'

The couple left. The priest knelt down by his empty

fireplace and remained there for a long while on his red knees, but he did not pray.

Some months passed. It was in the brief autumn, when the snows were coming down like curtains over the distant mountains, when the fisherman reappeared at the priest's house. The priest was busy with an old shepherd who had walked a long way to seek consolation; when he finally entered his parlour, he was unprepared for what he saw.

The fisherman looked much as ever, although there was a pale blue ribbon tied round the hat he clutched, and an autumn flower tucked beneath the ribbon. But the transformation of the servant girl, who stood beside him, was complete.

Grana's face was painted, her dark hair curled. She wore a little shawl over her head. Her costume consisted of a silk blouse with a gold-embroidered jacket over it, a fully-gathered skirt-like garment, separated and sewn like trousers, and elaborately decorated and pointed slippers. This sumptuous costume was adorned with filigree jewellery and ornaments. An elaborate necklace studded with semi-precious stones hung round Grana's neck.

The priest had never seen anything so beautiful. Envy rose to his face and coloured his cheeks. He understood that this wedding costume had probably been in the fisherman's family for generations, and was worn only for such occasions. But it bestowed on Grana such a queenly grace that, in one single blink of his eye, the priest saw all that his holy calling had demanded he give up. He felt himself half a man.

When the priest had mastered his feelings, he conducted the ceremony in the nearby church. It was a simple ceremony, since the fisherman and his bride had rowed across the lake alone, bringing no friend from the poorer village. As witness, the priest called in his boy, who overnight had become a gawky adolescent with a deep voice and an inability to look anyone in the eye.

After the ceremony, the traditional sweet jams and wines were eaten and drunk. The newly wedded couple went to the quayside and climbed into their humble boat, to the bows of which a sprig of green laurel had been tied. Then they rowed away across the lake to the poorer village.

The best part of another two years passed before the fisherman again rowed himself across the lake. As he stepped ashore, he might have seen – had he been so minded – a most unusual sight in the more prosperous village. For, drawn up in the little square, was a motor-car, with a lot of brasswork and a large headlight. It was the first motor-car ever to penetrate to this part of the world. The twentieth century had come to the more prosperous village.

But the fisherman went direct to the priest. The priest was in his church.

The fisherman told the priest that his wife was dying and had asked that the priest come across the lake to give her a last blessing.

A flame leaped up in the priest's eyes and died.

'No one from our village visits yours. The lake is too dangerous on your side.'

'God will protect you. Grana needs you, Father.'

The priest stopped only to get his hat and his cloak, and then he hurried beside the fisherman to the quayside.

He sat hunched in the bows of the boat while the fisherman rowed with slow, untiring strokes. The waters of the lake glided by, becoming blacker. The more prosperous village began to shrink, to look small, slight, negligible; the mountains, on the other hand, stretched their black flanks and began to dominate all that lay below them. The sun was swallowed up by the teeth of the mountains. A chilly wind blew, and waves splashed spitefully against the planking of the boat.

From the level of the water, the poorer village looked poor indeed. The houses were of stone, their roofs were of stone. They merged with the background. There was no colour anywhere. As they drew nearer to the fisherman's jetty, however, a splash of saffron appeared. A woman ran out of the fisherman's house and waved to them.

They reached the jetty. The fisherman secured his boat and helped the priest ashore. There stood Grana, smiling happily in a saffron dress. She threw her arms about her husband.

The priest folded his arms and looked furious, suspecting some evil trick. The couple persuaded him to enter their house, where a wood fire burned. There Grana explained that she had become convulsed directly her husband had gone, and had vomited up a fruit stone which had stuck in her gullet. Immediately she had felt better. Now she was her old self again.

Although he nodded his head a few times, the priest remained surly. But the fisherman and his wife were all happiness, and insisted that he must stay the night with them, since darkness was already falling.

The priest did not know what to do. He walked outside and looked longingly across the lake, where the more prosperous village was fading into night. He felt he was on unholy ground; superstitious fears filled him. Behind the house, on the folds and slopes of the mountain, wolves called to each other. But it was clear he could do nothing but stay, which he did with as good a grace as he could muster – and was treated to a superb trout for supper, washed down with rich white wine.

Afterwards, the couple gave him their wooden bed to sleep on, above the pen where the nanny goat lived in the winter. They slept in the other room, beside the embers of the fire. The priest lay awake for a long while, staring into the dark, listening to the slap-slap of the lake outside, alert to hear if any noises came from the couple.

Next morning, the fisherman rowed him back across to the other side of the lake.

Several months passed. One day, the priest's man, who had sprouted a thin beard, encountered the fisherman coming from the quay. He led him to a farmhouse, where the priest was consoling an old woman whose mother had just died.

'I'm not coming across the lake again,' said the priest, frowning.

'Grana is dying and asks for you, Father,'

'So you said once before.'

'She has given birth, Father, and is dying. She begs you to come.'

'And you?'

'I also will beg if begging is what pleases you.'

They stared hard at each other. Then the priest went to get his hat and coat.

This time, it was no false alarm. In giving birth to a strong boy, Grana had caught a fever. The priest and the fisherman arrived too late. Grana was dead. She stared blankly up at the roof-beams until they closed her eyes.

The priest said his blessings over the corpse. Then both men, pale-lipped, went outside. One went behind the house, one stood in front. Both wept, the priest silently, the fisherman aloud, with great cries of pain forcing themselves from his chest.

The priest slept that night by the dead fire. The fisherman slept by the dead body.

Next morning, they rowed across the lake to the more prosperous village, to bury Grana in sacred ground, in the shadow of the priest's church.

The priest conducted the ceremony with great feeling. Afterwards, when the fisherman was about to return to his boat, the priest said to him, 'Your business with our village is now finished. You will not need to visit here again. Farewell, and stay on your own side of the lake.'

The years passed, season gave way to season, and on the heights of the far mountains the snows came or receded.

When the fisherman once again rowed himself across the lake, he saw that the more prosperous village had extended its quayside, and a modest building in pink stone had been erected nearby. Flowers of a brightness he had never seen before grew in its flower-beds. On the front of the building was a sign reading, Grand Hotel. Two cars and a smart carriage-and-pair stood before its open doors.

After a moment spent gazing at these wonders, the fisherman proceeded to the house of the priest. The priest had some grey hairs in his beard. He recognised the fisherman at once, and stood up, though without uttering a word of greeting. A plump woman who had been in the room with him faded silently away into the kitchen.

'My son Vuk is now eight years old,' said the fisherman. 'He is old enough to think as a man, and he has decided that he wishes to be baptised in the faith of his mother. Will you accompany me across the lake to perform the ceremony?'

'Why did you not bring the boy here? I have crossed that lake twice, back and forth, in my life, and that is sufficient.'

'My son has friends in our village. He wishes them to witness his baptism.'

The priest sat down in his chair, put his hands on his knees, and looked up at the fisherman. 'Do you think me mad?'

'You might convert everyone in our village if you came.'

After a long pause, the priest sighed and reached for his hat and cloak. This time, he took a scarf as well.

The poorer village had not advanced over the years. It had become more dilapidated. The minaret, the tallest structure in the village, had fallen down in the last high wind of winter. Its stones were being used to patch the houses of the villagers, or to serve as steps up to the pasturage. Black curly-haired pigs wandered through the village, sheep bleated behind it. The priest baptised little Vuk hastily, and then persuaded the fisherman to row him back home again before night fell. A wind was getting up, and the surface of the lake was uneasy, turning like a drunken man in his sleep.

'Vuk's a fine boy,' said the fisherman.

'He reminds me of his mother,' said the priest. He was feeling ill.

Nine years, almost ten, passed. It was summer. There had been a war. Rumours of it reached even to the poorer village on the west side of the lake, while the more prosperous village on the east side had been badly treated. It had been incorporated in a new nation and was made to fly a flag of hitherto unknown design. Several of its wealthier citizens had disappeared mysteriously. The Grand Hotel had closed, to open later as the Town Hall. From its balcony the strange flag flew. A small motor boat bearing the same design of flag took to speeding up and down the lake, patrolling an invisible barrier.

The fisherman rowed himself across the five miles of water and tied up at the quay. A uniformed man asked him what he wanted and demanded to see his passport. The fisherman, not knowing what to say, was dragged off to the Town Hall for interrogation.

Eventually the police there acceded to his request, and summoned the priest to identify him.

The priest looked a lot older. There were locks of white in his beard; his shoulders were bowed. He walked with a stick. He had gone with the army during the war, and had been beside the soldiers when they fought in the country in the south, where – it had once been rumoured – the women were extremely beautiful and expert with their oily cuisine. The rumour was false: there was only bitterness and hard biscuits in the south, and many a good man had died. The priest himself had been wounded in the leg.

Wearily, cautiously, the priest admitted that he knew the fisherman and would vouch for him. Rather than leave the man in the cells, he agreed to let him spend the night at his house, on the understanding that the fisherman would return to the other side of the lake in the morning. If he ever came back, he stood in danger of being shot as a spy.

There was a fat, bustling woman at the priest's house. The priest patted her bottom and called for a jug of wine and some food. He sighed, sank into a chair, and rested his damaged leg on a log situated nearby for that purpose.

'How's your boy?' he asked, when the wine was poured.

'Vuk is well. He is a shepherd. He is engaged to a girl, and they wish to marry.'

'No,' said the priest promptly, seeing what was coming. 'I can't do it. It's impossible. It's forbidden.'

The fisherman said nothing more.

After a long silence, the priest said, 'You see, things have changed. We're a new nation. They don't much like priests, I can tell you that. It's forbidden to cross the lake.'

'You're glad of that,' said the fisherman. 'You hate me, don't you, Father?'

21

'We must put aside hate, my son, and love one another, as God commands . . . Yes, I did hate you. I don't any longer. I'm a different man. I don't understand you, but I don't hate you. Why don't you and Vuk and his sweetheart come and live here? You can go to church. You can fish. It's a better place than your broken-down village.'

After a while, the fisherman said, 'We don't have any uniforms, or police. Why don't you come and live with us? You would make many converts. Perhaps what we need is a priest, religion, belief . . . '

The fat woman came back into the room, beaming and bearing two plates of food. The priest and the fisherman ate at the table in silence.

'Good food,' said the fisherman, as he pushed his empty plate away.

'Not as good as the trout you once served me.' After a pause, the priest said, 'Give me a while to think over your offer. I want a quiet life. Let's see how much worse things get here. Could I bring *her* over too?' He gestured in the direction of the kitchen.

The fisherman nodded. 'I must owe you something, Father, some kind of debt. I'll come back in a year or so, by night, and see how you are getting on.'

'Be careful, then. People have been shot. One here, in the village. And several in the hills. New nations are difficult. Uncomfortable.'

Next morning at dawn, the priest accompanied the fisherman to the quayside, just to see that there was no trouble. The motor boat was already patrolling offshore. Builders had begun to knock down a row of old houses.

'They will build a bioscope there,' said the priest. 'To show us all some propaganda films. To put me out of business. That's progress.'

'The fish swim on both sides of the lake,' said the fisherman.

They shook hands for the first and last time.

The winter came, the snow line crept down the distant mountains. The surface of the lake grew black and, when not black, white and grey with its annual visitors, the geese. With spring came the storks, flying northwards to longer days, and nesting on the roofs and chimneys of the more prosperous village; that was still not forbidden. A new police post was built on the road that ran out of the village and along the lake. The telephone line came over the hills, but led only to the police post and the Town Hall. Bread was rationed. Posters appeared everywhere, announcing that everything was going to be better.

Shooting was heard up in the hills, and out on the lake.

The priest was sleeping in his soft bed with the fat woman when there was a knock at his outside door. In the old days, he would have called out reassuringly and hurried down to greet whoever needed consolation. Now, a midnight knock filled him with fear. He threw on his clothes, seized his stick, and went slowly downstairs. The woman, not daring to light the oil lamp, sat upright, shivering in the bed.

Conquering his hesitation, the priest opened his door. He could hardly make out the dim figure standing in the darkness.

'Father, let me in and bolt your door, if the door has a bolt.'

The priest recognised the accent as that of someone from the poorer village across the lake. He let the stranger in, bolted the door, made sure the shutter over his one window was secure, and lit a candle.

A handsome youth of under twenty years stood on the opposite side of the little flame. The resemblance to Grana was so strong that the priest recognised him at once.

'Vuk!'

The young shepherd put out a large rough hand and shook the priest's hand.

'I'm sorry to frighten you at this hour of night. It's impossible to cross the water by daylight.'

A fear came to the priest's heart.

'Your father?'

The young man said, 'He was coming to see you. He made you a promise. He chose a moonlit night to row over. The motor boat was out on patrol and they saw him.'

'They shot him? We heard shooting on the lake.'

Vuk nodded. 'They hit him in the chest. Father feigned dead. When they had gone, he managed to row himself back to the shore, using one oar. I found him in the morning, as near to death as a man can be, the blood drained from him into the bottom of the boat.'

'And now?' He leaned forward anxiously, staring into the eyes of the young shepherd.

'For five days he has lingered in the mazes between life and death. He wants your blessing. I came when it was dark enough. I'm sorry, father.'

'No, it's all right.'

They stood silent for a minute. A dog was barking distantly. The priest blew out the candle. They stood patiently together in the thick murk of the room.

'Father, there's a message for you, too. Whether he lives or dies, my father says that his house is yours.' As if he understood what was in the priest's mind, he added, 'I've my own house. I built it when I married.'

'You also need a blessing, Vuk.'

They stood together, silent. There were footsteps outside, low voices. In his fear, the young shepherd reached out and held tightly to the priest's sleeve. But the steps went by, dying into silence.

'You're needed on the other side of the lake, Father.'

'I'll come,' said the priest, with a sigh.

24

As before, he put on his hat and his cloak, and wrapped a scarf round his neck. This time, he also went upstairs and packed a bag with a couple of books and some clothes. He came down slowly in the darkness, and the fat woman, dressed and well wrapped, came down with him. Vuk held the door open and they stepped out into the night air.

The Gods in Flight

Behind the hotel, cliffs rose sheer. The steps which had been cut into the rock long ago made their ascent easy. Kilat climbed them slowly, hands on knees, and his small brother Dempo followed, chattering as he went.

At the top of the climb, the boys were confronted by huge stones, fancifully carved in the likenesses of human beings, water buffalo, and elephants, all squatting among the foliage crowning the island. Kilat clapped his hands with pleasure. A hornbill fixed Kilat with its pebble eyes, flapped away, and glided towards the sea. Kilat watched it till it was out of sight, pleased. The bird was popularly supposed to be a messenger from the Upper World, and was associated with the beginnings of mankind.

'That hornbill can be a sign that the world is not destroyed,' Kilat told his brother. Dempo tried to climb up a negroid face, planting his bare brown feet on the negroid lips. He still carried baby fat, but Kilat was eight and so lean that his ribs showed.

Kilat stood on the edge of the precipice and stared in a north-easterly direction across the gleaming waters. The sea looked calm from this vantage point, one of the highest on the island; silvery lanes wound across it reflecting the morning sun. Further out, a leaden haze absorbed everything.

Shielding his eyes, Kilat searched in the haze for sight of Kerintji. Generally, the peak was visible, cloud-wreathed, even when the long coast of Sumatra remained hidden. Today, nothing could be seen. Kilat loved Kerintji and thought of it as a god. Sometimes he slept up here under the stars, just to be near Kerintji.

Although he stood for a long time, Kilat saw nothing in the haze. Finally he turned away.

'We'll go down to town now,' he called to Dempo. 'Kerintji is angry with the behaviour of men.'

Still he lingered. It had always been his ambition to get on a ship or, better still, a plane, one of the big white planes which landed on the new airfield, and go north to see the world. Not just the nearby world, but that huge world of affairs where white people travelled about in their white birds as if they were gods. He had already started saving his rupiahs.

The two boys made their way back down the steps. His mother sat on the front steps of her hotel, smoking and chattering to her servants. There were no tourists, no white people, although it was the season for them to arrive, so there was no reason to work.

When Kilat was not made to do small jobs about the hotel, he sold rugs and watches down by the waterfront. Today, it was not worth the effort, but he stuffed some watches in his pocket, just in case.

'You can stay here with me,' their mother told the boys. But they shook their dark heads. It was more interesting down in the town, now that they were growing up. Kilat took his brother's hand to show his mother how responsible he was.

The road into town wound round the hill. Going on foot, the boys took a shorter route. They walked down flights of stone steps which, according to legend, the gods had built to allow the first man and woman to climb out of the sea. Every stone was carved; did not steps too have souls, waiting to find expression through the soles of man?

The sun was already hot, but the boys walked in the occasional shade of trees. They had a fine view of the airstrip at one point, stretched like a sticking plaster on one of the few flat areas of the whole of Sipora. All was quiet there. Heat rippled over the runway so that its white lines wriggled like the worms dogs spewed.

'Why aren't the white planes flying?' Dempo asked.

'Perhaps the gods are not coming to Sipora any more.'

'You mean the devils. It's better if they don't come, Kilat. No work for you and mother, isn't that a fact?'

'It's better if they come.'

'But they spoil our island. Everyone says it.'

'Still it's better if they come, Dempo. I can't tell you why but it is.'

He knew that it was something to do with that huge world of affairs which began over the horizon. The schoolmistress had said as much.

As they negotiated the next section of stairs, the airport was hidden behind a shoulder of rock. Butterflies sailed between Upper World and Earth. The stairs twisted and they could see the little town, with its two big new hotels which were rivals to his mother's hotel. The Tinggi Tinggi had only six wooden rooms and no air-conditioning. The new hotels were of concrete; one had twelve bedrooms and the other sixteen little bungalows in its grounds. Among the trees behind the bungalows a part of the old village was preserved; its saddle-backed longhouses stood almost on the shore among the palm trees. Their roofs were no longer of thatch but corrugated iron which shone in the sun.

'The old village is excitingly beautiful,' Kilat told his brother. He kept some brochures under his mattress which he saved when his mother's tourists threw them away. One of them had described the village – he had asked the schoolmistress what the English words meant – as 'excitingly beautiful'. It had completely changed Kilat's appreciation of the longhouses. Not that he believed them to be beautiful; he preferred the sixteen little concrete bungalows; but the words had mysteriously distanced him from what had once been familiar. In the photograph in the brochure, the longhouses on their sturdy stilt legs did look excitingly beautiful, as if they no longer formed a part of Sipora.

The steps finished where the slope became easier. Cultivation began immediately. Water buffalo were working in the fields, together with men, women, and some children. A Chinese tea-seller walked along the top of an irrigation dyke, his wares balanced at either end of a pole. Everything looked as normal, except that the tourist stalls which dotted the sides of the sandy road to town were shuttered and padlocked.

'This is where the white gods buy film for their cameras,' Kilat said, indicating a stall where a Kodak sign hung. He spoke crisply, with assumed contempt – yet in a curious way he did feel contempt for these rich people who came for a day or two and then disappeared for ever. What were they after? They made so much noise and became angry so easily. They were always in a hurry, although they were supposed to be on a 'holiday'. It was beyond Kilat to understand what a 'holiday' was. The elders said that the tourists from the north came to steal Sipora's happiness.

'They won't need any film now,' Dempo said. 'Perhaps they have taken enough pictures.'

'Perhaps their own gods have stopped them flying in their planes.'

They had both watched tourists photographing, jumping up and down and laughing as they watched, to see the way these lumpy people always pointed their cameras at the same things, and the most boring ones. Always the water buffalo, always the longhouses, always the tumbledown coffee shop. Never the sixteen little concrete bungalows or the airport.

In the market square, they met other boys. Dempo played with his friends in a ditch while Kilat talked and joked with his. The weekly boat from Padang should have arrived this morning at nine, but had not done so – Kilat had looked for it from the mountainside and noted that it was missing. The world was mad. Or possibly it was dead. Just as the gods had created Sipora first, perhaps they had left it till last. Everyone laughed at the idea.

Later, George strolled by, as usual wearing nothing but a pair of rolled-up jeans and a battered hat. He was German or American or something, and he lived in a cheap *penginapan* called Rokhandy's Accommodation. George was known locally as The Hippie, but Kilat always called him George. George was about as thin as Kilat.

'I'm heading for the airport, Kilowatt. Like taking my morning constitutional. Want to come along?'

'Kilowatt' was just George's joke – not a bad one either, since Kilat's name meant 'lightning'. Kilat always enjoyed the joke, and he started walking beside George, hands in pockets, leaving Dempo to look after himself. He took long strides, but George never moved fast. George did not even have a camera.

They skirted the shore, where the wind-surfers lay forlorn with their plastic sails on the sand. Rokhandy himself, bored with the failure of his business, was sailing out on the strait, almost to where the wall of purple cloud began. George waved, but received no response.

'Seems like the good ole Western world has finally

31

done itself in for sure. For fifty years they been shaping up for a final shoot-out. There's the lore of the other West, Kilowatt, old son, the one where the cowboys ride the range. Two brave men walking down Main Street in the noonday sun, one playing Goodie, one playing Baddie. They git nearer, and they don't say a thing and they don't change their expressions. And then – bang, bang – the fucking idiots shoot each other dead, 'stead of skedaddling off down a side alley, like what I'd have.'

'Were you a cowboy once, Georgie?' Kilat asked. The Hippie went right on with his monologue.

'I feel kind of bad if that's like what's happened in real life. I'd say *our* President and *their* President seen too many them cowboy films, they finally put pride before common horse sense once too often – 'n' this time all the bystanders they got themselves killed as well. Serve 'em right trusting the sheriff. So I feel kind of bad, but let me tell you, Kilowatt, old son, I also feel kind of good, because I used to warn 'em and they took not a damned bit of notice, so finally I skedaddled down this here side alley. And here I still am while bits of them are flying up in the clouds like snowflakes.' He made a noise like a laugh and shook his head.

Some of this Kilat understood. But he was more interested in the lizards climbing over the cowling of the tourists' speedboats, beached like dead sharks. The man who ran the speedboats was sitting in the shade of a tree. He called to Kilat.

'Why don't you take a ride yourself, like Mr Rokhandy's doing?' Kilat asked him. 'I'll come with you. I'd like a ride.'

'Got no fuel', the man said, shaking his head. 'No power. The oil tanker didn't come from Bengkulu this week. Pretty soon, everyone is going to be in trouble.'

'He's always complaining, that man,' Kilat told George, as they walked on.

The haze was creeping over the water from the north, where the sky was a livid purple.

The Hippie said nothing. He kept wiping his face with a dirty rag.

'I'm feeling low. I never trusted no sheriff ... Jesus ... '

The airport was close now. They had merely to cut through the Holy Grove to reach the broken perimeter fence. But once they were in the shade of the trees, George uttered a sound like a muffled explosion, staggered to a carved stone, and threw himself down on it at full length.

'Rokhandy's wine is really bad,' he said. 'Not that I complain, and after all Rokky drinks it too, so fair's fair. All the same ... Jesus ... ' He sat up, rolling himself a joint from a purse full of the local *ganja*. 'Suppose those cats have truly done for themselves this time round. Those big political cats ... '

Kilat sat and watched him with some concern. There were many things The Hippie did not understand.

'You're sitting on the tomb of King Sidabutar, George. Watch out he does not wake up and grab you! He's still got power, that old man. You're one of his enemies, after all.'

'I'm nobody's enemy but my own. Jesus, I love old Sidabutar.' George gave a slap to the warm stone on which he sat.

The stone formed the lid of an immense sar-cophagus, shaped somewhat like a primitive boat, ter-minating in a brutal carved face. The blind eyes of this face gazed towards the new airport and the mountain behind. Other tombs and menhirs stood among the trees. None was so grand as the king's tomb. Yet almost all had been overcome by the spirits of the trees.

These tombs were ancient. Some said they had existed since the dawn of the world. But the story of King Sidabutar was as solid as if itself carved in stone.

The people who lived on Sipora had once been part of a great nation. The nation lived far to the north, even beyond Sumatra, beyond Singapore, away in the Other Hemisphere. The nation had then been prosperous and peaceful; even the poor of the nation lived in palaces and ate off gold plate. So said the legend, so Kilat told it to George.

George had learnt patience. He lay on Sidabutar's grave and stared into the shimmering distance.

Powerful enemies came from further north. The nation fought them bravely, and the names of the Twelve Bloody Battles were still recalled. But the nation had to yield to superior numbers. Led by King Sidabutar, it left its homes and moved south in search of peace. Thousands of people, women and children along with the men, deserted their ancestral grounds and fled with their animals and belongings. The cruel invaders from the north pursued them.

There was no safety for them in the south. Wherever the beaten nation went, it was assailed. But the great-hearted king always encouraged his people; by force and guile he persuaded them to remain united against everything. They came at last to the sea. They crossed the sea, thanks to intervention by the gods, and settled in Sumatra, the Isle of Hope. Even in Sumatra, head-hunters and other ferocious tribes made life miserable for the king's people. While some of the nation moved into the forests and mountain ranges of the interior, the king himself, accompanied by the ladies and gentlemen of his court, again crossed over the seas. So he came at last to the peaceful and fruitful island of Sipora.

By this time, King Sidabutar was an old man. Most of his life had been spent on the great journey, whose epic story would never be forgotten on Earth. When he reached the shelter of what is now the Holy Grove, he fell dying. His queen tended him and wept. The old king blessed the land and proclaimed with his dying breath that if the enemies of his people ever landed on Sipora, then he would rise up again in majesty, bringing with him all the Powers of the Upper World in vengeance.

'What a guy to have for a hero!' exclaimed George. He lay smoking his joint and looking up into the branches of the *hariara*, or sacred oak. The oak's roots had spread and widened, taking a grip on the king's sarcophagus with arms like veins of petrified lava.

'Sidabutar is the greatest hero in the world,' Kilat said. 'You ought to get off his grave.'

'Sidabutar was a bum, a real bum. One of the defeated. He got his gang kicked out of wherever it was – somewhere up on the borders of China, I guess – and spent his whole life on the run, right? Always heading further south, out of trouble, right? Finally he freaked out here, on this little dump of an island in the Indian Ocean . . . Jesus, Kilowatt, that's the story of my life. Do you think some cat's going to be loony enough to raise up a stone tomb for me? No way. Old Sidabutar is just a plain bum, like me. A plain bum.'

Kilat jumped up and started pummelling George in the chest. 'You bastard! Just because you screw old Rokky's daughter every night, I know! Don't you say a word against our king. Otherwise he will fly right up and destroy you *flat*, just like America and Russia have been destroyed.'

George rolled out of his way and laughed. 'Yeah, maybe, maybe – and destroyed for the same good reason. Talking too much. OK, man, I'll keep my trap shut, and you keep Rokky's daughter out of it, right?'

Kilat was not satisfied. He was convinced he could sense King Sidabutar's spirit in the Grove. The curious thing was, he felt the same uncomfortable mixture of admiration and contempt for Sidabutar as he did for the white gods. If they were so clever, how come they ruined everything? If the king was so great, how come he let them ruin everything? They had brought gonorrhoea and other diseases to Sipora – the old king did nothing about it.

But he said no more, because Dempo came running through the trees. Between complaints that his big brother had left him, Dempo had a long story to tell about a *beruk* monkey escaping while climbing a coconut tree.

'Never mind,' Kilat told him. 'We are going with George to the airport. It's excitingly beautiful.'

George nipped out his joint and they made their way through the sacred oaks, each one of which looked sinuous enough to contain a living spirit.

Since there was no traffic, the airport guards had gone home. Nobody was about. They were able to walk right across the runway, across the magic white lines. The asphalt was hot to bare feet. Lizards scuttled away into holes as they went.

In the foyer of the airport building, two rows of floor tiling had been taken up and a trough chiselled in the concrete beneath, deep enough to take a new electric cable. But the cable had not materialised, and the trough lay like a wound across the empty space. Upstairs, a good many locals were gathered, to admire the view, to chat and pass the time. The kiosk was open, selling beer.

In the side window of the kiosk, a two-month-old newspaper had been hung. The paper was yellowing, the edges curling like an old leaf.

Under a headline reading SUPER POWERS END IT !!! was a report from Manila, describing how the long-anticipated nuclear war had broken out between the countries of the Warsaw Pact and the NATO Alliance. It was believed that Europe was destroyed. The Soviet Union had also fired its SS20s against China, who had not retaliated. The USA had made a massive retaliation, but was herself destroyed. The entire northern hemisphere was blanketed in radioactive dust-clouds. Manila was suffering. Nobody had any idea how many people had died or were dying. The monsoons were bringing death to India.

George glanced at this document and laughed bitterly. 'If the poor old kicked-about planet can fix its circulation system properly, odds are on staying safe here in the Southern Hemisphere. Just don't let them ship in any of that radiation muck down here.'

They talked to a lot of people, but only rumours could pass between them. Some said that Australia had been destroyed, some mentioned South Africa. Others said that South Africa was sending hospital teams to Europe. Kilat enjoyed just being in the lounge, with its map of world communications in marquetry on the wall. He felt powerful in the airport. This was the escape route to other lands, if they still existed.

'Will we be wiped out?' Dempo asked. 'The white gods hate us, don't they?'

'No, nonsense. We are the lucky ones. The great body of Sumatra lies between us and all that destruction. Kerintji and the other giants will keep infection away from us.'

He thought about his watches, and walked among the crowd trying to sell them. Nobody was in the mood for buying. One smartly dressed merchant said, shaking his head, 'Watches are no good any more, my son. Time has run out.' He looked very sad.

The airport siren sounded. An official in the uniform of Merpati marched into the lounge and addressed them. He held his hands up, palms forward, for silence.

'Attention. We are receiving radio messages from a plane in trouble in the area. We have signalled it to land in Bengkulu, but there is trouble in the plane –

illness of some sort – and they are running out of fuel. The plane will land here.'

A babble of questions greeted the statement. Men pressed forward on the official. He was a middle-aged man with greying hair. He smiled and waved his hands again as he backed away.

'Do not worry. We shall deal with the emergency.' His words were drowned by the siren of an ambulance, swinging out of its garage on to the tarmac just beyond the reception lounge. 'We ask all those who have no official business here please to quit the airport premises for their own safety. The plane is larger than the types officially designated to land here. We may have a little trouble, since the runway is too short in this instance. Please vacate the premises immediately.'

More questions and excitement. The official held his ground and said, 'Yes, yes, I understand your worries. No worries if you do not panic. Please evacuate the building peacefully. We understand the plane is American, bringing high-ranking officials from San Diego.'

At the word 'American', the panic got under way in earnest. Everybody started to run, down the stairs or simply round the lounge.

Kilat grasped Dempo's hand and charged downstairs. They elbowed their way out through the double glass doors. They had lost The Hippie, but Kilat did not care about that. He ran with Dempo, aiming for the airport fence. The fire engine went by. When he looked up he saw the sky had hazed over. It felt suddenly cold.

Someone whistled. The boys looked and saw George leaning against the open doors of the ambulance garage. He beckoned them over.

They ran to him; he stooped to put his arms around them.

'Sounds like there might be a little excitement. Let's wait here. I want to get a look at these guys getting off this plane.'

He stared hard at Kilat, saying, 'Heap bad medicine, Kilowatt.'

He relit his joint, his soft face unusually grim. Kilat and Dempo squatted in the dust. They could look right across the airport to the Holy Grove, and through the Grove to the sea, its surface sullen, no longer glittering.

'To see a plane come in from here will be excitingly beautiful. Have you ever been to San Diego, George?'

'If these cats survived, they have been underground, out of harm's way.'

Kilat did not understand, and allowed himself to be cuddled only a minute. But he remained close to George.

After a while, George said, 'Listen, Kilowatt, these cats are going to bring trouble. Plenty trouble. If they survived the holocaust and they've grabbed a plane, then they are bigwigs, that's sure. And if they come this far – like why not some place nearer home? – then it figures that some other guys along the way would not let them land, right? I'm telling you, these cats may be loaded with marines and God-knows-what, like bodyguards. They bring trouble.'

'They'll – perhaps they'll be grateful to us . . . '

'Grateful, shit. Cats with guns aren't grateful. They'll be looking for one last shoot-out.'

'Maybe it's the President of the United States coming to visit us,' Dempo said, hoping for reassurance. He looked frightened and clung to George's leg.

Kilat said in a small voice, 'You think they might take Sipora over?'

'Why not? Why the hell not? I know these cats, think they own the world. Maybe your police should gun them all down as they cross the tarmac.'

Kilat looked concernedly up into The Hippie's face. He could tell George was frightened. Overhead, the engine-roar grew slowly louder. The plane remained hidden in the overcast.

'We've only got six police and they've only got one gun between them. They're just for controlling tourists, that's all.'

George looked wildly about. 'Maybe the damned bird will crash if the runway's too short. Blow itself up and good riddance. We need those cats here like we need the clap.'

Dempo started to jump up and down. 'Oh, I hope it crashes! I hope it crashes! That would be really excitingly beautiful.'

The airport was now a scene of wild action. Sirens were blaring, and people and cars were moving about the runways. The island's one police car was trying to hustle them out of the way. Centreline lights came on along the landing strips; high-density approach lights, white touchdown zonelights, winked on. Flags were rushed up masts. More people were running up from the direction of the town.

Suddenly the noise of the plane was louder. The plane emerged from the low cloud. It was enormous, silver, predatory, its undercarriage unfolding. It made the universe vibrate. Anyone sleeping anywhere on the island would have been awakened.

Dempo and Kilat fell over in awe.

The plane came roaring down, aiming straight for the ambulance shed, or so it appeared. Then, with a gust of wind which curled the dust off the airport, it was gone again. They saw its glaring jets before it vanished back into the cloudcover.

All the people out on the airport ground had flung themselves flat. Now they got up and ran for safety, while the cars drove off in all directions, revving their engines and skidding to avoid collision.

'It'll be back,' George said. He spat on the ground. 'Pilot just took a look. His instruments must be malfunctioning. Who the hell could those guys be up there? Oh, I don't like this, I don't like this one little bit.'

'It's the President, I know it,' Kilat shouted. He had to shout. The noise grew greater. The plane had turned over the strait and was coming in again.

'Run slap into the mountain, you bastard!' George called, raising a fist to the sky. 'Leave us in peace.'

They saw it then. This time it was much lower, spoilers up, ailerons going down, nose lifting. The undercarriage appeared to brush the tossing palms at the far end of the field. It looked too enormous and fast possibly to stop in the length of the island.

'Crash, you bastard!' George yelled as it rushed by, monstrous, bouncing, jarring. Grit whipped up into their faces. The scream of the tyres hit them. Then it was past.

It was slowing. Only a few hundred yards to go to the far fence. Both the ambulance and the fire engine were roaring along behind it.

The plane juddered as it braked while the fence came nearer. Now it might stop in time. But momentum carried it on. Stones flew.

Still thundering, the silver monster ran over the threshold markings, bumped off the end of the asphalt, and crunched through a row of flashers. The people watching through the wire fence broke and ran.

The machine swerved, rammed a wing against the fencing and ploughed in a leisurely way through the side fence, striking its nose and one engine against palm trees. Part of the undercarriage snapped. The plane sank to one side as if going down on one knee. Smoke, steam and dust covered the scene.

'Jesus,' said George.

'Jesus,' said the boys in imitation.

The scene seemed to hold as if time had frozen. The diffused sunlight made everything shadowless. Then one of the emergency exits opened in the side of the plane. A yellow escape chute billowed out.

Passengers began to slide down the chute, one every one and a half seconds. They came down like dolls, only returning to life at the bottom as they picked themselves up. The smashed engine was smoking. Suddenly it burst into flame. Flames ran along the wing, rose up over the cockpit. Shouts came from the plane, another exit opened forward of the wing, uniformed men jumped out and fell.

'Wouldn't you know it – soldiers!' yelled George. 'The Yanks are coming.'

He started hurling abuse at the men lining up beside the yellow chute. They wore battle dress, helmets, and were armed with machine carbines.

The two boys could see that most of the men were in bad condition. Their faces were pale, their hair patchy. Some were bandaged. Some fell to the ground directly they exchanged the air-conditioning of the plane for the muggy atmosphere of Sipora. Although the fire was gaining hold, and their movements were panicky, the newcomers moved slowly and stiffly.

'They are ill,' Kilat said. 'They are bringing their diseases here. Let's skedaddle down a side alley . . . '

'There ain't no more side alleys, son.'

As the fire engine drove up, the soldiers stopped it, aiming their weapons at the crew. Black smoke billowed across the tarmac.

Older men were now deplaning. They walked painfully towards the airport buildings. Most of them wore peaked caps with braid, and medal ribbons on their chests. An armed escort fell in and accompanied them, carbines at the ready.

'It's the fucking Chiefs of Staff!' George yelled.

'Those are the bastards that started this war, and they think they can hide out in some damned bolthole in the Indian Ocean.'

'They have the sickness,' Kilat called, but George was already running out of the shelter, running across the concrete towards the approaching column of decrepit figures, swerving to avoid the oily smoke.

Kilat saw it happening, saw the muzzles of the guns go up, saw the faces of the soldiers. He never forgot the faces of those soldiers. They tightened their mouths, froze, became expressionless, and fired. Fired at George as he charged towards them shouting.

The bullets came spanging in the direction of the boys. Kilat pulled Dempo to the floor as one smacked into the back of the garage. When he looked up, George had fallen and was rolling over and over in a curious way, kicking his legs. Then he stopped and lay still.

Even as George ceased to move, another noise added itself to the roar of fire.

It was a quite distinctive sound, like a whistle, like a giant's exhalation. The ground shook with it.

Among the trees opposite where the boys lay, clouds of steam billowed up. They concealed something rising from the earth itself, from a gaping tomb. A great figure grew taller. It came up like a rocket. Its head emerged above the crowns of the trees in the Holy Grove.

Smoke and steam wreathed that countenance like whiskers, but the expression of an anger implacable in intent was clear to see.

King Sidabutar had woken at last from his long sleep. He rose like vengeance, to summon up the Powers of the Upper World. Science was dead: now he was free to wreak destruction on his enemies.

The Blue Background

To the north stretched the line of the Carpathians, unvisitable. Although the mountains could be seen from almost every hut in Drevena, they played little part in the lives of the inhabitants; this contemporary generation did not believe even that demons lived in the mountains, as their forebears had done throughout countless generations.

The little River Vychodne flowed through the village, and perhaps formed the main reason for the hamlet's being where it was. A crude waterway system had been set up – no one remembered by whom – to help irrigate the stony land cultivated by the peasants of Drevena; for the land flooded in winter and became dry in the hot summer months. The sea lay a long way distant: no man of Drevena had ever set eyes on the sea and returned to tell of it; so that its moderating influence could not alleviate the harsh climate of the region.

On the outskirts of the village stood a ruin, still referred to as the House. It had been considerably grander than the rest of the poor buildings, and its stones were still mined to patch walls. Since its destruction, which even the oldest inhabitant, spitting into his fire of a night, failed at some length to recall, nobody grand, or with any claims to grandeur, lived in Drevena. Only the poor remained, stranded in the middle of the stony land, compelled to earn their living by tending the reluctant soil.

Beyond the ruin of the House was a hut where the Lomnja family lived. Poverty in Drevena was fairly shared, but the Lomnja family were poorer than any of their relations. Old man Lomnja had been partially blind since youth; his wife, Katja, was frail, good-hearted but improvident. Of the six children she had borne to Lomnja three survived, a boy, a girl, and a younger lad, Lajah. All of the work on their sparse acreage was shared, though the brunt of it fell on the males, Lomnja and his two sons, Hlebit and Lajah.

Just as the home of the Lomnja family was furthest from the centre of the village, so their holding was furthest from the River Vychodne.

The exact characteristics of their land were familiar to all the family; they worked it over ceaselessly throughout the seasons.

The family had a cow named Marja. Marja spent the night in a small lean-to stall tacked on the back of the Lomnja dwelling. Every morning, weather permitting, she was driven down a narrow track to the family holding.

The holding began after a creaking wooden bridge, which was no more than a few planks laid across a shallow ditch. The land consisted of three ridges sloping towards the west, where they became one. This western end was most fertile; stones had been extracted from it over the ages and a wall built with them, to keep Marja out. A few vegetables, lettuces, radishes, spring onions, tarhuna, and green peppers grew there.

On the rest of their land, the Lomnjas grew potatoes, mainly on the lower ridge, and barley on the two upper ridges. Beyond the ridges was wild land where nothing flourished but patches of grass and occasional wild sage bushes. There Marja was left to forage while the others worked the soil.

The landscape in which they bent their backs was austere. The mountains were distant in one direction, often lost in cloud. In the other direction lay flatness, bisected by the dusty road which led from nowhere to nowhere and passed through Drevena as it did so.

There was another landmark nearby.

On the middle strip of land tilled by the Lomnja family stood an ancient ruined church.

Most of the church roof had fallen in; the dome had collapsed, perhaps in the time of the Turk, over two centuries ago. But the walls still stood, and against the south wall old Lomnja grew his vines. Katja and her husband made a few barrels of wine every year, wine acknowledged to be the best in the village. The small income they gained from the wine kept the family together.

All that the ruined church meant to the family was a windbreak; it provided a sheltered place in which their precious vines could grow. Only to little Lajah did the church mean something more.

Lajah was a dark, undersized, skinny lad with black questioning eyes – just like all the other boys in Drevena. He wore an old jacket of his brother's and a pair of trousers, and he went barefoot most of the year, even when snow lay on the ground. He worked no better than any other boy. He was no more intelligent. He was not especially handsome. Since he never spoke much, he was not regarded as particularly bright, and in consequence he was not much spoken to, even by his contemporaries. His old grandmother, who had died last winter, when the wind from the east was at its height, had talked to him, telling him old dark legends, and had taught him ancient songs. Yet he could not even sing particularly well.

Lajah loved the decrepit church. He did not care about poverty; poverty was a natural condition. He was proud to be a Lomnja, because the Lomnjas had the old church on their land.

Every day, when the family rested at noon, sitting with their backs against the ruinous southern wall to eat their blinis (and a bit of cold fish if they were lucky), little Lajah would enter the church by the broken door and stand among the weeds and rubble.

The space inside the church seemed large to him. Nothing of the landscape outside could be seen. The clouds formed the roof. He climbed over the rubble and stood at the far end, where once an altar had stood.

Here, a portion of roof still overhung. It sheltered an old wooden figure secured with arms outstretched to the wall. The boy would look up at it open-mouthed, until his father called him back to work.

'Who put the figure there?' Lajah asked his father.

'It's Kristus.'

'But how long has it been there?'

'I don't know, do I?' responded his father. 'Centuries. Before the Turk. Stay away. The building is dangerous.'

In the centre of the village was a hut, almost as humble as all the rest, which served as a meeting place. There the men smoked their pipes together and sipped a little tea or wine or pear water. Sometimes, they spoke of Christ. Sometimes they spoke of Mahommet. But the names came out with a deep peasant contempt, exhaled among blue smoke, as if they had no substance. Christ and Mahommet had come and gone. The land had remained. And the people had remained to farm it. Whoever the gods were, whoever the lord was, what was important was the state of the crops.

'Neither Christ nor Mahommet could put up with

life in Drevena,' one old man said, and the rest of the group chuckled.

Lajah was listening with his elder brother, Hlebit.

'But Christ's still here in the Lomnja church,' he said.

More chuckling. One of Lajah's uncles said, with kindly contempt, 'That's just an old stick of wood with the worm in it, lad.'

Lajah's brother punched him in the ribs.

Next day, Lajah went back to the church and looked again at the figure hanging on the wall. It moved him deeply. Christ had his arms outstretched, and the arms were too long and did not fit properly to the body. His body was thin, like an old peasant's. He wore only a brief garment over his lower body, the folds of the cloth crudely indicated by the carver. His legs hung down like two sticks.

The head of Christ was turned to one side with a simple gesture of pain. His crown of thorns was carved almost carelessly, so that it looked as if his head was bound about by rope. His mouth hung open in a human despair. He looked rather stupid, as if the woodcarver, for all his piety, was unable to imagine intelligence.

'Christ must have been a peasant too,' Lajah said to himself.

What also moved him was the ancient and faded colouring of the figure. The body was yellow and cancerous with age, as if Christ were already far gone in leprosy when crucified. His garb was carmine, the colour still clinging in the deeper folds, his hair brown, his face a mottled red and brown.

These simple earth pigments stood in contrast to the blue background against which Christ's figure was set.

The crucified Christ had no cross. Wood was scarce in these parts. The distorted capital T of his figure was nailed against the plaster wall of the church with rusty iron spikes.

The wall was knotted and lumpy. However long ago it had been plastered, it still retained the impression of carelessly applied downward brush strokes. The pigmentation had once been deep blue. Now the richness of that colour lingered only where the timber body afforded it some protection from sun and rain; elsewhere, it had faded to a delicate sky tint, a blue that spoke of seas and distant eternities.

It was to this background as much as to the figure that Lajah directed his gaze. It seemed to him that Christ was stepping forward from the blue of Heaven. When the sun shone in, the shadows of the stiff arms endowed Christ with spectral wings, blue on blue.

Nothing of what he felt could the boy declare, so he said nothing even to his sister. He worked beside his elder brother and his father in silence.

A day came when summer was advanced, and the grape harvest nearing. The distant line of the Carpathians had lost their caps of snow. Katja was picking the first fruits from their apricot tree when she espied a man on horseback, distant, tremulous in the heat.

In wild excitement she ran out to the small-holding to tell the family. They straightened their backs and peered when she pointed. Even old Lomnja shaded his eyes and looked, though he could see no further than the end of his beard.

There on the road which bisected the olive green landscape was a man riding a horse, even as Katja claimed. He must be coming to the village – no avoiding that, as the road unrolled – and maybe he would stop. Surely he would stop. Perhaps Drevena was his destination.

They all laughed at that idea, even old Lomnja,

because it was difficult to see why anyone should want to come to Drevena.

'Perhaps he's heard tell of our wine, father, and wants to sample it,' Katja said to her husband.

All round them, sparsely dotted about, the rest of the population of Drevena stood upright in their fields, flexed their backs, and stared towards the dusty road. As if by common consent, all began to trudge towards the village. The crops would not die for want of an afternoon's attention. Strangers were worth investigating.

When the stranger arrived in Drevena's one street, the whole village – every man, woman, child, and dog – was waiting for him. The sun was low by then, and he cast a long shadow as he dismounted from his mare.

The men of Drevena were not certain how to greet strangers. They remembered a time some years ago when 'the army' – as they called the platoon which had appeared one winter – marched through Drevena on Franz Josef's business. Then they had wisely taken to their heels and hidden in the fields. To this solitary man, they merely doffed their hats and waited for him to speak.

'Greetings, my friends. I am a traveller. Miltin Svobodova by name. I have come a long way and still have far to go – to Ostrava, in fact. Your village does not look very hospitable, but heaven knows how far it is to the next one, so I have decided to stay here for the night. The Lord God will guard me.'

The man's accent was so astonishing, as was what he had to say, that no one could answer him. The men huddled together and discussed with each other. Eventually, one of them said, 'What makes you think you can stay in our poor village? Suppose we decide to beat you up and rob you, God or no God? You've a strange fancy to come to a place like this on your own, haven't you?'

51

'I take you for simple Christian folk, as I am myself, and expect no harm from you, since I offer you no harm.'

The man was quite slender, pale of face, dressed in black, with a silk hat on his head. He confronted them in a confident way, though without swagger.

'There's nowhere fit to sleep in Drevena. Nor do we have anything to do with religion. Ride on down the road. It's only two hours to Goriza Bistrica. That's a better place. Everyone says so.'

'My mare's too tired to go further. I shall pay for my lodging – more than the miserable billet is worth, no doubt.'

At this, they conferred again.

The cottage in the middle of the village which served as a meeting place was an inn of a kind. There lived old lame Varadzia, who had Turkish blood; he was prevailed upon to make such accommodation as he could for the traveller.

The villagers peered in through the one curtainless window of the cottage. There they watched Svobodova unload his two packs, from one of which he brought a mysterious rosewood box with a handle and a pipe of some kind protruding from the front of it.

'No doubt he keeps his jewels in there,' said one of the more imaginative peasants. 'Perhaps we should cut his throat and share them out between us – then we'd all be better off and I could buy a cart. No one would ever hear of the crime.'

'Franz Josef would hear of it,' another answered.

After Varadzia had served Svobodova with sturgeon and the local delicacy, a hatchapuri – a sort of paratha stuffed with cheese – washed down with a glass of the Lomnja red wine, he sat down and took a pipe with the stranger. After a while, he let in a few cronies, all eager to hear what the traveller had to say about himself.

Svobodova talked grandly of life in Bratislava, of the beauty of its thoroughfares and churches, of the loveliness of the Danube with its bridge, and of the singing in the cathedral.

'What about the loveliness of the women?' Varadzia asked, boldly.

'That's not for Christian men to dwell on,' said the traveller, severely.

'I'll bet they're a sight more attractive to look on than our lot, though,' one of the peasants remarked.

Changing the subject, Svobodova spoke of the rest of Europe beyond the Dual Monarchy, of how powerful Germany and Great Britain were, the latter with vast possessions overseas. And of how brilliant was the organ in Notre Dame cathedral in Paris, though the city was notorious for its sinfulness – almost as bad as Prague in that respect.

'So I suppose you have come to these arid parts to escape from the sinfulness, sir,' said Lajah's father. 'Almost no trees grow near Drevena, so sin is sparse also.'

'I am a photographer,' said the stranger. 'That is God's will. Happily, I have private means, and I travel about recording a vanishing way of life with the new photographic equipment. I am convinced that Europe is becoming too steeped in the flesh, and that the Lord in his wrath will soon punish her with a war more terrible than any before, waged with all the modern weapons at our command. So I travel throughout our country, compiling a record of what is and may not remain for long.'

'Nothing's going to change here, you have our word, sir. Life goes on here as ever. We can't even afford a new bridge. We'd never have a war here.'

'That's as may be,' said Svobodova. 'Now I wish to sleep. In the morning, I shall photograph anything here you consider of significance.'

The men looked at each other uneasily over their pipes.

'We've nothing here of any significance, depend on that,' they said, as they took themselves off to their flea-ridden homes.

Next day, the sun rose in majesty from its mists, and the inhabitants of Drevena went out before the heat arrived to tend their acres. They ignored Svobodova, having decided that he was a harmless madman. Anyone who considered that there was anything in Drevena worth photographing was mad.

Svobodova stood in the middle of the road in the middle of the village and photographed the road. He photographed the ruins of the House. He photographed Varadzia standing self-consciously before his doorway.

'You'll do better in Goriza Bistrica, down the road,' Varadzia said. 'It stands on the edge of a gorge and its houses were built in the Turkish time. Besides, there are priests and things there which would appeal to you.'

'I'll be on my way, then,' said the photographer. Settling his account with Varadzia, he loaded up his mare, carefully stowing the precious camera in a pack, and set off down the dusty road.

As he went his way, figures straightened up one by one in the fields and stood like statues to watch him. It was as if they speculated on the sights he would see beyond the horizon. Then they shrugged and turned their heads down towards the earth again, almost with the gesture of cattle grazing.

Svobodova was aware that a small boy was running towards him over the broken terrain to the right of the track. The boy grew nearer and for a while ran parallel with the track, on the far side of the babbling Vychodne. When a bridge came, the boy crossed it and ran in front of the man on his slow-moving mount.

The photographer halted his mare and looked down at the boy without speaking.

The boy was about thirteen years old, as far as Svobodova could judge. He wore an old tunic-jacket, a pair of baggy trousers, and very little else. He looked up at the man with an open and trusting expression, and asked, 'Did you photograph anything important in Drevena?'

Svobodova rubbed his chin.

'Everyone told me there was nothing worth photographing in Drevena. You people are not very proud of your village, are you?'

'There's one important thing you must photograph.'

The boy turned and pointed back across the fields to where the church stood, vines growing up its southern wall.

'Well, my lad, unfortunately ruined churches are two-a-penny in Slovakia. What's important about that one?'

'Inside, sir, come and see. The important thing is inside.'

Miltin Svobodova was kind-hearted as well as principled. He imagined that the Lord might have sent this boy as a messenger. Without arguing, he climbed from his saddle; he followed Lajah across the fields and his mare followed him.

Lajah led him to the old broken door of the church, where Svobodova tied up his horse. Boy and man entered the ruin together, while the rest of the Lomnja family straightened their backs and watched this strange event open-mouthed.

At the far end of the shell stood the ancient wooden Christ against its blue background. Lajah led the man forward without a word.

When they were near enough, he simply stood and gazed upwards. The stiff medieval figure remained, recording the agony of spiritual man; the shadow of the broken roof was high at this hour, cutting across the coarse texture of the blue wall and shading the roughly carved head of the sufferer.

The photographer crossed himself, bowing his head before the ancient symbol.

'Here is the true spirit of this harsh, godless land,' he said. 'God may be despised, ignored, but he is never absent. This poor representation, quite untouched by Renaissance values, was doubtless carved and painted by some dumb serf such as that fellow outside, to express an inner light struggling for expression. That inner light, my boy, is the one hope for our sinful world.'

'But it's beautiful, isn't it, sir?'

Svobodova looked down at Lajah, head on one side, and then permitted himself to smile.

'It's certainly worth a photograph.'

Lajah watched as the magic box came out and the photographer prepared his plates. On the top of the box, which was of rosewood, an oval plate was affixed; on it were embossed the words 'London Bioscope Co., 1911'. He scarcely listened while Svobodova worked at setting up his tripod, explaining as he did so that a firm of publishers in Vienna and Bratislava had commissioned him to produce a volume of photographs of rural Slovakia. If the photograph of the Christ figure was successful, it would appear in the book.

A deal of fussy preparation followed. The boy became bored. Christ remained as he had been through the centuries, hanging cankered from the old wall. Finally, the shutter of the rosewood box clicked and the picture was taken.

'I'm grateful to you, my lad,' Svobodova said, as he stowed away his things. 'You are the one spiritual person in a heathen village. You represent the hope and the future of Drevena. Now, let me write down your name and address in my notebook and I will see that you receive a copy of my book when – the Lord willing – it is published.'

It was done. He remounted his mare, gave a farewell wave, and headed for the delights of Goriza Bistrica. He was never seen in the area again. For a while his visit was talked of – since there was very little else to talk of – and then he was forgotten.

Lajah grew to manhood and married a girl called Magdalena, who was known to cook a delicious stew. For a few weeks, life for them was paradise; but the demands of toil eroded the edge of their happiness. There was no freedom from the fields. They became just another couple. Soon, there was little to mark them out from the rest of the villagers, except that Lajah still made infrequent excursions to the ancient church to look at the timber in its anguished gesture against the blue wall.

Winter came. Magdalena carried Lajah's child. The winds blew from the east, loaded with the destructive fury of winter. The distant pass was blocked by snow. Drevena was cut off completely from the outside world. The villagers stayed in their poor huts, shivering and starving.

Spring brought heavy rain. One morning, when the peasants waded out into the fields to plant their crops, or salvage what was already planted, they found the church had collapsed. The old wooden figure of Christ was buried under the rubble.

'It had been there a good long time, mind.'

'Long before the time of the Turk, they say.'

A few days later came the post waggon, carrying letters and passengers for Goriza Bistrica. The pass was clear again. On its rare appearances, the waggon stopped always at Varadzia's, where the driver paid well for a bottle of Lomnja's red wine. On this occasion, the driver handed over not only a silver coin for the wine but a parcel heavily wrapped in cloth and addressed in large letters to Lajah Lomnja.

'What do you think it could be?' Magdalena asked, excitedly, and Lajah turned it over and over, admiring the stamps. 'It has come all the way from Bratislava just for you, Lajah. I didn't know you knew anyone there. You are a one for secrets, and no mistake.'

At last they opened the parcel. They knelt on the stone floor over its contents. Inside was a large impressive book with padded covers. The mauve cloth was emblazoned with gold lettering which read, 'Scenes of Rural Slovakia – Our Vanishing Heritage, by Miltin Svobodova.' The edges of the pages were gilt.

Lajah turned the pages with clumsy hands. There were many pictures. They meant nothing to him. Nor could he struggle to decipher the text underneath.

Towards the end of the book, he came on a photograph of something he recognised.

It showed the Drevena Christ, the Christ now vanished, the spindly Christ nailed to the old wall, arms outstretched, head to one side in a toothless grimace of pain.

Lajah put his finger on the photograph and said to his wife, 'I was there when the man came to Drevena and made that picture. See, it's part of the old ruined church that collapsed in the last rainstorms. I used to go and look at it when I was a kid.'

She stared at the picture and at him. He said nothing more. Leaving the book lying open on the floor, he went outside. His hoe leaned against the mud wall of the building. Taking it up, he went back into the fields, sparing never a glance towards the pile of rubble which marked the site of the church.

As he bent his shoulders towards the soil, he

thought with contempt of the foolishness of that photographer who had come long ago. A city man. He had photographed the old timber figure, certainly. But his photograph was in sepia. It failed to capture the blue background, the glimpse of infinity, that Lajah had once loved, before life closed in.

Igur and the Mountain

On the first day of September, in an earlier century, a child was born of peasant parents. He was named Igur. On the second day of September, his mother set him on the step of her cottage in a wooden cradle, where the sun shone on him. On the third day of September, snow began to fall.

Igur grew up a strong young lad, and full of a natural intelligence, although there was no school in Kackavalj, the village into which he was born. From an early age, he accompanied his father into the rough pasturage round Kackavalj to look after the sheep on which the villagers depended.

He soon came to understand the harsh limitations binding life in Kackavalj. The village perched on top of a mountain. The descent down the mountainside, amid bushes of azaleas and stunted oaks, took half a day or more. Only one point was higher than Kackavalj, and that was Mount Elbruz, whose snowy peak loomed to the south, and whose profile was often concealed by storms which later played about Kackavalj itself.

'When you can't see Elbruz, it's snowing. When you can, it's about to snow.' Such was the bitter joking wisdom of the people of Kackavalj, whose stock of proverbs served instead of schooling.

Young Igur needed no school in which to learn the facts of life on the mountain. Summers were short, lasting for three months only. The snow that had settled on his new-born nose was no freak event; for the first of September marked a beginning to the long nine months of Kackavalj's winter. This was the central fact of life for those who lived in Kackavalj; it shaped all their thoughts and their actions.

Igur was a merry lad, and a sturdy one. During his adolescence, the harshness of life scarcely touched him. He could not understand why his seniors complained so much. Even when summer arrived, they went in terror of the next winter, soon to come, or groaned about the one that was past, or about extra bad ones only they remembered, when their sheepdogs froze solid whilst waiting to be let in the door.

When summer came, Igur forgot about the cold, and celebrated.

'Celebrate the first day of summer, lest you get no chance at the second.' Such was another cheerful saying in Kackavalj.

And on the first of June, the whole village – or those able enough – fell into a state of rejoicing for a week.

Kackavalj had no resident priest. There was a church. It perched above the village in ruinous condition, a relic of the days before the Turks, but few visited it except old widows, who climbed its path like black beetles on holy days, to worship at its mouldering altar. Priests have to look after themselves, so the old priest who had Kackavalj in his care lived down at the bottom of the mountain, where the climate was more merciful.

The old priest's name was Alexis. On the first day of June each year, he saddled up his fat old mule and left Kackuss, the village at the bottom of the mountain, heading for the village at the top. Once there, he set up shop in the little main square of Kackavalj and opened the annual celebrations; which is to say, he performed a mass marriage, uniting in wedlock all those boys and girls who had fallen in love with each other during the long months of winter.

Primitive musical instruments were brought out, wine was poured, enormous mutton pilaus were served, and all the brides and bridegrooms, and everyone else in the village, made merry for seven days. On the eighth day, they all went back to work again. Then old Alexis blessed the parish, saddled up his mule and departed down the mountainside, winding through azalea and oak, for Kackuss.

So the years passed in Kackavalj. The winters came and went, and the chill winds blew.

'Keep warm while you can – you're a long time dead.' Such was a favourite greeting among the shepherds, if they met of an evening in one or other's cottage for a drink.

In the conversations of Kackavalj, one topic took precedence even over winter and weddings: sheep. Everything depended on the hardy mountain sheep, whose hides were tough, whose fleeces were thick, and whose flanks were thin. Mutton dominated the diet as lambs did the talk.

Day or night, fair or foul, the flocks had to be watched in their scanty pastures. In the long dark nights of December, the shepherds would wrap themselves in immense cloaks made from departed members of their fold, and crouch, red-eyed, over a small fire. Their duty was to frighten off wolves which would otherwise have fallen ravening on the sheep. The blizzards would whistle and roar from the glacial top of Elbruz, and the cry of the wolves would rise above the cry of the wind.

Sometimes the wolves would become desperate with hunger and attack the men.

It happened that, when Igur came of an age to

marry, one wolf in particular was known to the shepherds. It too, by some chance or other, was called Igur. Igur the wolf had a black muzzle; perhaps his mother had not been a true wolf. Igur the Wolf was especially feared because he had been known to speed into the village in the light of day, to snatch a human baby from its cradle as it lay defenceless.

Igur the Man developed a strange bond with Igur the Wolf.

Whenever Igur the Man had to take his turn in the snow-streaked night, to watch the flock, there somewhere beyond the pale of his fire would be Igur the Wolf, watching him. Igur would take up his staff and drive the wolf off, but man and animal often came close, confronting each other as if they were tied to each other as man and wife.

'Fear the wolf when he ceases to call.' Such was a local motto.

And one dreary night, when Igur the Man was out with the flocks, the old wolf Igur ceased to call. A cold wind blew from the east. Igur took shelter in the lee of a boulder. A small fire, into which he fed some last branches of fir, burned at his feet. The sheep huddled together close at hand. Close above their heads was cloud, boiling across the bleak slopes of the mountain range.

Igur looked up. Green wolf eyes glared down at him. Igur the Wolf had climbed to the top of the boulder and was preparing to spring. Igur moved. Too late. The wolf fell upon him. They rolled together by the flickering fire. The sheep took flight and ran.

The snapping jaws of the wolf were almost at Igur's throat. Its hot breath fanned his cheeks. Feeling with one hand, Igur managed to pull a branch from the fire. He brought it up and drove it into the thick coat of the predator.

Igur the Wolf gave a cry of rage and pain. It fell

away, coat ablaze. Howling, it ran for safety. As Igur climbed trembling to his feet, still clasping the brand, he saw the wolf make away up the slope. Its coat flamed. It disappeared, then could be seen more distantly. It disappeared again behind some broken stones. Then it was seen again, more like a spark in the storm than a living thing. Then it disappeared and was sighted no more. Nor was it ever seen again near Kackavalj.

One of the other shepherds had witnessed the battle between man and animal, and told the story in the village next day, with embellishments. Igur became the hero of the hour.

And more than the hour. On the coldest night of the year, the old mayor of Kackavalj fell stone dead as he drew on his night clothes to climb into bed. The people of Kackavalj had long felt they needed a younger mayor, one more able to deal with their problems. Accordingly, the next day, they made Igur mayor.

'To be a leader of men, one must subdue animals,' was one optimistic local saw.

Igur was in love with a girl who lived in a cottage two doors away from his own. Her name was Irini, and thought of her bright smile and dark curls could warm the chilliest night. Irini looked favourably on Igur, and never more so than when he moved to the mayor's house in the middle of the village, where there was a decent stove for warmth.

But Igur the Mayor made several discoveries, one of which was that he was now so busy listening to people's complaints that he had no time for courting.

Another discovery was how fixedly everyone's thoughts, winter or summer, centred round sheep. Winter, sex, sheep: there were no other considerations than these to be had in all Kackavalj. Even when rare visitors came to Kackavalj in the summer – Alexis the priest from Kackuss or the tax-collector from distant

65

Banjaflis – people utterly destitute of sheep – they would be greeted with the traditional Kackavalj greeting, 'May your ewes proliferate!'

Nor was this preoccupation with sheep surprising when one contemplated the nature of Kackavalj, and its reason for being where it was.

At the lower end of the village stood a tumbledown old building, larger than the rest, which had once served as a barracks for troops during Ottoman times. This was where the women worked every day of their lives, except during the week's marriage festival in June; in consequence, it was where Igur the Mayor had to go every morning of his life to sort out various quarrels and disputes.

In the Barracks – as the building was still called – the women worked upon the fleece of the sheep. Here the wool was washed and dried and dyed and carded and combed and all the other things that have to be done with the intractable material which, through an accident of nature, grows on the backs of ovine mammals.

One half of the Barracks was given over to three crude looms, fashioned out of local timber. On these looms, the women wove their dyed wool into crude bright rugs and carpets. The patterns of the rugs were traditional, and contained various symbols, the meaning of which had long since been forgotten. Here Irini worked, and was considered one of the best weavers, since her fingers were so nimble.

Each year, on the eighth of June, which is to say, as soon as the long winter and the week of wedding festivities were over, the women would pack up their carpets. They would load up the half-dozen starved mules belonging to the village. And they would proceed down the mountain, winding slowly among the oaks and azaleas. Starting out at dawn, they would arrive at the bottom of the mountain, and enter Kackuss some time in the afternoon.

Kackuss was a modest place, well-favoured with springs, and sheltered from the fury of Elbruz. It lay in the midst of its pastures and watercress beds, and it possessed two large hans or inns. At these inns, depending on the season of the year, you can count on finding merchants from distant Banjaflis.

The merchants from Banjaflis are there, comfortably established in the hans, when the women from Kackavalj arrive. There they sit, smoking comfortably on their balconies. Most of the carpet merchants are fat and smiling. They sport gold rings on their fingers.

The women and their mules arrive in the courtyards of the hans. They unload the animals and unpack their goods. They display their rugs, the produce of the long winter, in the yard. Then they sit down and wait. They look up at the merchants, and whisper to each other that the merchants idling above them have vast fortunes accumulated in distant Banjaflis.

Slowly, the merchants from Banjaflis notice the women. They begin to stand at the rail on the balcony. The women lift their red, shining faces and call out impatiently, 'Don't you want to buy? What's the matter with you?'

'Your stock looks like poor quality trash,' one merchant will respond, and then the bargaining begins.

Eventually, a deal is done. The women are always dissatisfied with the price they get, the merchants with the price they pay. All the women's complaints go back to the mayor of Kackavalj. As for the mayor of Kackuss, he sits back and is entertained by the merchants.

The women sleep that night in the stables of the han. Some of the older ones get drunk; some of the younger ones get pregnant. Some get robbed. All enjoy a little excitement, according to temperament.

'Kackuss, where every snow flake has a price tag . . .', as they say at the top of the mountain.

Next morning, it is a sad story. The women round up their mules and climb the winding path that leads to home. Meanwhile, the carpet merchants are chuckling to themselves and preparing to leave for distant Banjaflis with their spoils.

When the women arrive back in Kackavalj, towards evening, the men are waiting for them. They have a blanket spread in the middle of the little square. They stand rigid and grim-faced.

'How much money did you get?' they demand.

Then the women lament loudly. They gesticulate towards heaven and cry out that they were robbed, and that the people of Kackuss are thieves, and the merchants of distant Banjaflis bigger thieves. After much protestation, they pull what is left of their pay out of their blouses and fling it defiantly down on the blanket.

The men count it, and then set on the women and beat them.

There is a saying in Kackavalj, 'The wife carries her husband on her face; the husband carries his wife on his back.'

After this expedition of the women was over, it was Igur the Mayor's business to sort out all the quarrels that resulted.

Igur was possessed of both tact and patience. These qualities were taxed to the utmost. The amount of money the women brought back on the ninth of June was vital to the fragile economy. A few roubles could make the difference between mere hunger and starvation during the lean months of the year.

Whatever he did, it seemed Igur was always blamed for the rancour that followed on the quarrels. Far from being united in their difficulties, the people of Kackavalj were inclined to quarrel over the little they had. 'The hard-up are hard-hearted,' as the proverb laconically states.

Worse still was to come on the fifteenth of June. For then it was that the men went down the mountain to Kackuss.

At the upper end of the village stood a dilapidated building called the Factory. It was the largest building in the village except for the Barracks. This was where the men of the village worked every day of their lives when they were not out on the mountain with their flocks. In consequence, it was where Igur the Mayor had to go every afternoon of his life to sort out quarrels and disputes.

In the Factory, the men worked upon the milk of the ewes. The ewes were milked into pans. The milk was allowed to turn sour. When semi-solid, the fermented milk was wrapped in blankets and boiled in giant coppers. The end product of this activity was a strong-smelling cheese called Galacknik. It was rubbery and considered to be at its best as a gastronomic treat when eaten hot.

Galacknik was a great traditional delicacy, made only in Kackavalj, and its fame had spread throughout the land. Accordingly, it commanded a certain price, and was much sought after in such sophisticated places as distant Banjaflis.

Each year on the fifteenth of June, as soon as the long winter was over, and the wedding festivities and the women's expedition were finished, the men would bring all their great round galackniks out of store and load them on to the half-dozen starved mules which belonged to the village.

They would set off at dawn, and proceed down the mountain. They whistled and sang as they went, filling the slopes with echoes. They emerged from the azaleas and oak trees to enter Kackuss some time in the afternoon.

There lay Kackuss, in the midst of its watercress beds and pastures. In its central square stood the two large hans. At these hans, on the fifteenth of every June, you can count on finding cheese merchants from distant Banjaflis.

The cheese merchants are comfortably established in their hans when the men from Kackavalj arrive. They sit smoking on their balconies. The cheese merchants of distant Banjaflis are lean sorrowful-looking men, who permit themselves never a smile as their customers arrive.

The shepherds tie up their mules and unload them in the courtyard. The round white cheeses are unpacked, and laid out temptingly in the sun. Then the men stand about and smoke, striking picturesque poses. Occasionally, they glance upwards, and remark to each other, out of the corner of their mouths, that these scoundrels idling above them have accumulated vast fortunes in distant Banjaflis.

At last, the cheese merchants affect to notice the shepherds below. They stand at the rail of the balcony. The men lift their red leathery faces and shout, 'Do you want to buy our cheeses this year or don't you?'

'There's no demand for cheese this year,' one merchant will reply, and then the bargaining begins.

Eventually, an arrangement is reached. The men are always furious with the price they get, the merchants sorrowful about the price they pay. All the men's complaints eventually go back to the mayor of Kackavalj. Whereas the mayor of Kackuss gets his cut.

The shepherds play merry havoc in Kackuss that night, drinking heavily, chasing the local women, and fighting with any men they come across – most of whom have had the sense to make themselves scarce. Sometimes, the shepherds are robbed, or imagine themselves robbed, and then damage is caused all round the village.

Next morning, it is a different story. The shepherds who were full of fight are now ashamed. Some nurse black eyes. Some have quarrelled with their best friends. They saddle up their mules in silence. Meanwhile, the cheese merchants, who prudently kept to their quarters overnight, maintain sorrowful faces as they prepare to leave for distant Banjaflis with their haul.

The shepherds ascend the winding paths that lead to home. They arrive in Kackavalj towards evening. The women are waiting for them in the square. They have spread a blanket in the dust. They stand with arms akimbo, faces grim.

'Let's see the profits,' they say.

The men look furtively at each other and rub their unshaven cheeks. One mutters that they were robbed, and that, as the women well know, the people of Kackuss are thieves, and the merchants of distant Banjaflis bigger thieves. After a lot of shilly-shallying, they drag what is left of their payment out of their pouches and fling it down shamefacedly on the blanket.

The women scream, count the money, and then set upon the men and beat them.

There is a saying among the females of Kackavalj, quoted often amid sighs at the loom, 'Smile at a man if you must, but laugh only with another woman.' On this occasion, the women neither laughed nor smiled. They knew there was a hard winter ahead.

When this male expedition was over, it was the duty of Igur the Mayor to sort out all the quarrels that resulted – and every household had a quarrel.

Igur used both his celebrated tact and his famous patience, which qualities were taxed to the utmost. The amount of money the men had brought back on the sixteenth of June was almost too little to pay the tax-collector, who was due to arrive in a week's time.

Whatever Igur the Mayor did, it seemed that he was somehow blamed for the rancour following on the

71

expedition to Kackuss. The inhabitants of Kackavalj quarrelled over the little they had instead of uniting in their common difficulty. 'Poverty makes faults solid as rock,' as the saying is.

So Igur called them all together and said, 'Friends, you know our wise old saw, "Kackavalj is founded on two things: a mountain and injustice." Well, we are stuck with the mountain, but I as your mayor am determined to do something about the injustice. Every year, we get robbed. I am going to saddle one of our mules and ride down to Kackuss. I shall go to see the mayor and speak to him man to man.

'I shall tell him that unless he refunds us a hundred roubles with which to pay our taxes, we shall next year take our goods straight to distant Banjaflis, and not stay in his rotten fleapit of a hamlet any more.'

This he said in a resounding voice, raising his arm aloft as if he were imitating a statue of some great military hero.

To his surprise, people laughed, and one man – it was Irini's father, too, which added to the insult – shouted, 'Don't be daft, mayor, we can never get as far as distant Banjaflis with our mules. We're forced to go to Kackuss.'

Igur the Mayor scratched his head a bit and thought. Then he said, 'Ah, but perhaps the mayor of Kackuss doesn't know that.'

He saddled up a mule and set off on his own. The people stood about dejectedly, without waving; then they went back to their sheep. What particularly upset Igur, as he wound down the mountainside among the azalea and oak, was that Irini was not with him. He had asked her to come, and she had replied saucily that if she did so her fiancé, to whom she had just become engaged, would be vexed with her.

An old saw kept returning to his mind as he rode: 'Women are beautiful, but only sheep can be depended on.'

Igur arrived in Kackuss in the afternoon. The mayor of Kackuss, who was asleep, had to be roused, while Igur waited outside on his doorstep. Unlike the village at the top of the mountain, Kackuss seemed to be full of idle men, who hung about eyeing Igur suspiciously.

When the big fat mayor of Kackuss appeared in his doorway, he scratched his belly and asked who his visitor might be at this time of day.

'I am Igur, the mayor of Kackavalj. I represent all my people, who have recently stayed in your village – '

At this, the fat mayor let out a noise between a bellow and a belch and said, 'So you're the one responsible for those louts up on the mountain! They caused two hundred roubles' worth of damage when they were here last week.'

Then he called to the people lounging in nearby doorways, 'Men, this impudent scoundrel is the mayor of Kackavalj!'

'Now, wait a minute,' shouted Igur, but the loungers descended on him and beat him up. When they had kicked him enough, they kicked him out of town, and he was forced to make his way up the mountain on foot.

In the night, he lost himself among the oaks and azaleas. As he wandered with the merciless stars above him, Igur consoled himself with one of the oft-quoted proverbs of the region: 'Strangers may attack you, but it's only blood relations who actually kill you.'

He staggered into the little square at dawn. Several people were about, munching hunks of black bread as they hurried to Factory or Barracks.

'How did you get on?' they asked.

'They stole my mule,' Igur said.

At this news, the people all set upon their mayor and beat him up.

The days went by. Igur tended sheep and went about his business. People would scarcely speak to him. Soon it was the day before the tax-collector arrived. That night, Igur lay in his bed, unable to sleep, wondering how the problems of Kackavalj would ever be sorted out. The tax-collector would come with soldiers in the morning. He would extract the tax demanded somehow, then he would depart again. But what would the villagers do in the winter? What would happen in the winter? How would they get through the winter?

Igur realised that he was growing old. Or perhaps he was just growing up. He understood now what had been a mystery to him in his childhood: he saw that the elders had reason to dread winter even in summer. Sure as taxes, the gaunt shadow of Elbruz would swing across the little village as the sun sank lower. The winds would blow again, the snows snow. In little more than ten weeks, winter would be upon them again in its fury, and the traditional suffering recommence.

Ten weeks was nothing. In boyhood, it had been an eternity.

He sat up in the dark and pulled on those boots of rams' leather which he wore in bed in the winter. He packed a little bag of belongings. He went out into the night, latching his door behind him.

The heat of the day had dissipated. It was very cold. Overhead, stars blazed as the eyes of Igur the Wolf had done, looking down at him without mercy.

Nobody was about. He went round to the stables and brought forth the best of the starved mules. He hoisted himself into the saddle.

As he rode down the street, he passed by Irini's cottage, and blew a kiss to its unlighted windows. He saw for the first time how miserable were the hovels in which they lived.

The mule seemed to know its course. It picked its direction slowly down the mountainside, brushing between the azalea bushes and oak trees. The mountainside was mysterious at night, as its giant shoulder moved over to obscure half the heavens.

He reached the village of Kackuss just before dawn. He did not pause as he passed the mayor's door. Instead, he prodded the mule on, seeking the track beyond the village. By the time the sun had climbed over the backs of the mountain range, he was firmly on the road to distant Banjaflis.

And there Igur the ex-mayor lives now. He has married a pleasant young woman and has two sons by her. He has not attained great distinction in that prosperous town, but his friends are many and his grey hairs as yet few. He has become a successful cheese merchant, and deals also in carpets, selling his wares in the remote capital for great profit. As he often boasts, he knows all the tricks of the trade.

When life is a little trying, as sometimes happens, Igur merely smiles, embraces his wife, and quotes to her an old saying he learnt from his elders during his childhood:

'In his heart, every man longs to die in a valley.'

Incident in a Far Country

A prince who lived in a far country had all that he
could desire, and one quality more, which brought
about his downfall. This is his story.

The prince was an exemplar of male beauty, with a
handsome face and figure, limbs of exceptional
smoothness, and a commanding presence. He glowed
with youth. He was an excellent marksman and
unrivalled in the hunt. Everyone agreed that the
strength of his physique was matched by the thrust of
his intellect, and he made many commendable
advances in astronomy and other sciences.

Except when hunting, the prince clothed himself in
white silks, dressing richly but simply. One glance
from his eye was enough to set women irresistibly in
love with him, whilst one frown terrified all men.

This power that the prince radiated found an echo in
the power of the state which he was due to inherit
from his father, the king. It was a favoured land, with
plains and forests to the south and mountains to the
north. The climate was good, with sun all the year
except for two periods in spring and autumn when the
rains came. Pure rivers ran through the land from
north to south. Wise government meant that the
frontiers were secure and the people, on the whole,

prosperous, kind, and contented. The prince was fond of travelling through the state with his advisers, solving the problems of his subjects; and all who met him loved him with a love in which fear primed their admiration, so great, so apparent, was the puissance of the prince.

People called him the Fair Prince, because of his handsome looks, though later the sobriquet acquired other meanings. Otherwise, the prince has no name, just as the quality which brought him trouble has no name: though some called it curiosity, or ambition, or perversity, or lack of imagination, or even – according to one wit – 'prince's itch'. It is strange that this quality, like the prince, has no name, since it may be readily observed in many men of ordinary station.

One fateful day, the Fair Prince was walking in the gardens of one of his northern palaces with a party of philosophers and advisers. The gardens were beautiful, being filled with birds and deer, as well as with exotic flowers grown from seed brought by caravans from distant regions.

The party came to a table laid with refreshment, around which sofas were placed. Gaudy umbrellas were held by slaves, to protect the Fair Prince and his company from the noon sun.

The Fair Prince seated himself. All present followed suit. They were refreshing themselves when one of the slaves who worked in the garden passed close by the party, carrying a spade over his thin shoulder. He passed so close that his shadow fell on the umbrella beneath which the Fair Prince sat.

Immediately, one of the prince's officials called for a guard, that the slave might be whipped for his effrontery.

'No, leave him,' said the prince, and he called to the slave in a kind voice. 'You have helped make this garden beautiful, and I am grateful to you.'

The slave was a man from the south, and very dark, with a skin roughened by work in the sun. He wore only a garment round his loins and a cloth about his skull. His shoulders had been bowed, in the manner of slaves everywhere, but now he lifted his turbaned head and looked straight at the prince.

It was said afterwards that his look was one of defiance. The prince took it merely as a look of *understanding*. Others thought the glance was supplicatory. The astonishing fact is that, despite thousands of years of practice, men and women still do not comprehend each other's expressions. Whatever this particular expression was – in itself such a small matter, yet of such significance – it was indisputable that for a slave to lift his eyes to a prince was in itself a gesture of gross impudence, punishable by death..

The slave made no answer to the Fair Prince's remark beyond that look. As he made off at a steady pace, there was more than one adviser who begged the prince to have the fellow executed immediately. They even went so far as to claim that if disobedience was not punished every time, as soon as it occurred, the whole social system would collapse. The prince made light of the incident, calmed his advisers, and proceeded to discuss whether or not, and in what sense, the world could be said to possess any external reality.

The slave's glance was not so easily dismissed from the Fair Prince's mind. It could be argued that, in the lists of external realities, it assumed a prominent place. Yet the prince had scarcely been aware of his slaves before this moment.

Now, wherever he looked, he saw that his kingdom was filled with slaves. Every second person was a slave. The numbers were highest in his own personal domains. Though he walked in perfect freedom, it was only because those about him were in captivity. Slaves prepared his bath and made his clothes and held his horse and cooked his meals and beat his tigers out of the bush and ran the palace and did a thousand other disregarded jobs too menial for free men.

Later on in the same day that the southern slave had met his gaze, the Fair Prince took himself for another walk in the palace gardens. He went alone – which is to say that his Chief Adviser remained some paces behind him, and kept quiet, for the prince could never be entirely solitary.

The prince walked with determination, and passed the spot where previously he had talked with the philosophers; slaves had now removed the furniture and the gaudy umbrellas. The path curved and sank. After crossing a wooden bridge over a stream, it began to alter character. It was no longer paved with marble, and its gravel surface soon gave way to sand. No banks of bright flowers fringed it. Instead, tall yews and cypresses grew, in some cases encroaching on the path. The path dipped further between rocks, and grew muddy.

As the way darkened, the prince encountered some slaves, male and female. They took one glance at the prince and then, recognising who he was, dived in terror into the bushes and made off like animals. However, their demeanour altered as the prince proceeded; far from jumping out of his way, they moved only reluctantly, averting their eyes and – he was sure – staring after him when he had passed, almost as though they considered him a trespasser.

Finally, the path ended among ancient and mossy olive trees, where a ramshackle building stood. Behind it was a cliff with rooms, or rather cells, carved out of it. At this point, the prince's Chief Adviser ran forward and said, 'Your Highness, this is where the slaves who tend your gardens live. I cannot advise you to go any further. Let us turn back. This place is too sordid for your eyes.'

Then the Fair Prince turned the full beam of his regard upon him, smiled, and said, 'But I'm going in.'

He entered the ramshackle building.

Several slaves were there, dressed in rags. Some rested, talking or spitting on the floor. Some smoked a vile weed whose acrid smoke assaulted the nostrils of the prince. When they saw who had entered their domain, they responded in various ways; but most of them, after their initial astonishment, shuffled away into the darkness.

One stooped old woman, with a brush of twigs tucked under her arm, came forward. With her gaze fixed on the cobbles before the prince's feet, she spoke respectfully, but nevertheless much in the terms of the Chief Adviser.

'I don't advise you to go any further, Your Highness. Turn back. This place is too sordid for your eyes.'

'Woman, fetch hither the southern slave to whom I spoke in the gardens this morning,' commanded the prince.

The old woman went off, muttering.

The Chief Adviser ventured into the stinking refuge, and said, trembling, 'Please be advised . . . ' But the prince stood his ground.

The old woman returned, still muttering, and spoke to the prince with downcast eyes, saying, 'He won't come. He's round the corner. You'd better go to him if you want him.'

'This is revolution,' exclaimed the Chief Adviser. He was middle-aged and inclined to be excitable.

But the prince merely shrugged and walked forward with his usual self-assurance. The floor became more uneven as he moved from the wooden building into the rock of the cliff. In a large chamber carved from the rock, he saw a number of huddled beings. The only light came from two narrow windows looking out on dark trees. The Chief Adviser shrank back from this den.

The slaves here did not move. As his eyes became accustomed to the dimness, the Fair Prince saw that the slave he was seeking stood near the middle of the room, leaning against a table. He looked as before, thin to the point of emaciation, his hands and feet white with dust, his body dark, his garment and turban torn. He regarded a point on the rock wall.

The prince said to him, 'I came here to find you.'

'Here I am.'

'I could have had you whipped this morning.' When he received no response to this remark, the prince understood that it might be construed as a threat and added, in amelioration, 'But you are a man the same as I.'

'I'm not the same as you.' For the first time, the slave turned his head and regarded the prince. His face was gaunt, the cheeks withered by sun and under-nourishment, so that his lips seemed tightly drawn against his teeth. His eyes were dark. He bore the full gaze of the prince without flinching.

The prince, who could answer almost any question the philosophers put to him, was puzzled to find himself at a loss to answer the slave. He said, lamely, 'At least I did not have you whipped.'

'Did you come here to tell me that?'

At these words – which again the prince found extremely difficult to answer – there was a stir among the occupants of the rock chamber. They sat upright and listened and looked. The Chief Adviser stood at the entrance of the chamber, his broad hand clamped over his mouth.

Throwing up his head, the prince said, 'I am indulging a whim to look at you more closely.'

'Well, now you see how we live, the slaves of your

gardens. In this den, forty of us have to make do, men and women, sleeping like animals on the floor, eating what offal gets thrown to us from the leavings of the royal table.'

The words were said dispassionately. It was the lack of passion, of anger, even of reproach, which moved the prince. He found himself saying, 'I will have a better place built for you.'

'And who will build it?' demanded the slave, with never a hint of gratitude in his tone. 'Other slaves?'

'Be grateful for what you are offered, dogs,' roared the Chief Adviser, finding his voice.

'Slaves know no gratitude,' shouted one of the men crouching on the floor. 'Our wages are whips.'

'I'll make you grateful, then,' said the Fair Prince, turning towards this new speaker. 'From now on, you will be paid for your work. I will see that you receive, each new moon, as much money as a guard at the main gate – or very nearly as much . . . '

His Chief Adviser grasped the prince by the arm. 'Leave here now, Your Highness, leave with me – you've surely said enough to this unruly mob.'

For the slaves were now rising to their feet, and several were calling out angrily that they worked harder than the guards and so should have more pay, or that they wanted whips abolished, or even that they should be released and allowed to return to their own countries.

As if unaware of the tabu broken by the Chief Adviser in touching the royal person, the prince turned with him to go, saying mildly, 'I will set things in hand. I see now that you have much to complain of, but you have a friend in me.'

'A friend! What a friend!' some slaves shouted, and the prince left the dismal place to general laughter, which mocked him long after he had returned to the palace.

That night, the Chief Adviser proceeded to the top of one of the towers, stood on the parapet, and disembowelled himself with two swift strokes of his jewelled dagger. His body was discovered by slaves early next morning.

The Fair Prince was gravely distressed by the suicide of his Chief Adviser, and distressed too by a note found on the body. The note was addressed to him. It made it clear that the Chief Adviser had died because he was guilt-stricken by his involuntary breaking of a tabu. The note added that the laws as established were there for good purpose, even when they seemed unjust, and that they had in most cases been established in previous ages, when men had a clearer appreciation of one another's natures. It ended by begging the prince to treat the slaves with firmness – in short, to have the lot of them beheaded before news of 'the disastrous occasion', as the note put it, spread to other slaves.

What the note did not say was that the Chief Adviser, before ending his life, had secretly sent a messenger on a fast steed to the king, informing him in detail of his son the prince's rash deed.

The prince summoned the rest of his advisers, and the matter of the slaves and the suicide was discussed at length. The advisers were one and all in accord, that traditions were there to be maintained, and that any change was for the worse. The prince laughed at them.

'The opposite is the case,' he said. 'If it was not for this foolish tradition that the persons of sovereigns are sacrosanct, our valued friend would not be dead today. His needless death is a proof of the stupidity of yesterday's law. I in no way objected to being touched by him, I scarcely noticed his touch. From now on, I pronounce myself touchable. Announce this new edict to my people forthwith.'

In fear of their lives, they pleaded with him. But that quality which has no name was growing strong in the prince. Thinking that he alone saw reason, he became deaf to their reasoning.

'Enough,' he said, turning on them a gaze full of the kind of puissance and beauty with which a tiger regards a fawn on which it has pounced. 'Any man may touch me from henceforth, and any woman. Slaves are men, slaves are women. They also may touch me. Such is my edict. I command you each to come forward and touch me.'

He stood there, alert, in his fine suiting. One by one, they filed by, eyes averted, cheeks burning with shame, and one by one they extended a trembling hand and touched the hem of his garment.

Despite his wisdom, because of his restless intellect, the prince could not understand the power of tradition. In consequence, he was more than surprised when, that very night, all the remainder of his advisers took the only honourable way out for men who have broken one of the most sacred tabus. But the prince was not granted much time in which to exercise his astonishment, for at dawn a delegation of slaves appeared at the palace steps.

The prince ordered the guards to sheathe their swords, and invited the slaves to enter, smiling upon them as he did so. He showed them into a luxurious inner sanctum, furnished with costly trappings, which had hitherto been reserved for councils of foreign ambassadors.

In this way, he hoped to please the slaves, but they immediately began to complain about the waste of money, which could have been better spent feeding widows and orphans.

'No doubt you are right,' sighed the prince. 'Now, what do you wish to talk about?'

The southern slave stood forth. He still wore his

ragged garb. He struck no particular attitude, simply shambling forward and addressing the prince as he would any other man.

'We've not come to talk. That's more your line than ours. We want some action. All yesterday went by and you never lifted a finger. Have you forgotten the deal we made the day before yesterday?'

'Oh, now, confound it,' exclaimed the prince, 'that was very far from being a *deal*, as you call it. I made a promise to you. Isn't that how it was? In any case, I was too upset to do anything yesterday; the chief adviser died.'

'We don't want a load of excuses,' said the southern slave. 'The agreement was that you would get us better premises, without any strings attached. Is that right or not?'

'Well, what I said was – '

'We all remember what you said, don't we, lads?' The slaves roared their agreement. 'So what we propose is this, seeing that you're so upset. To save you trouble, we are all going to move in here.'

'Move into the palace!' exclaimed the prince.

'Just turn all those concubines of yours out of the harem and we can settle in there right away.' He turned and started giving instructions to his companions.

'Oh, no, wait, look – think of the poor women – where will they go?'

'We're liberating them,' explained the southern slave. 'We look on them as our sisters, and count them among the oppressed.'

'Of course, we may keep a few of them for ourselves,' one of the other slaves said.

At this, the Fair Prince burst into a fury.

'This has gone quite far enough. Stop where you are or I shall call the guards and have you all beheaded. I will not have the palace treated in this way.'

The slaves, who were beginning to disperse, stopped in their tracks.

In the silence that ensued, the southern slave said, 'Call the guards, then. Go ahead.'

The prince did so. He strode about angrily, like one of his caged hunting cheetahs, until eventually a crestfallen captain of guards appeared. He saluted the prince. He explained that his men had heard that slaves were henceforth to be paid wages, and would receive almost as much as they did themselves. They had decided in consequence to go on strike until such time as fair differentials were established.

'Then we must set an example ourselves,' said the prince, in his rage. Seizing the captain's sword, he paced up to the southern slave and swung the blade, intending to lop off the man's head with one blow.

Everyone watched in silence. The southern slave tensed himself but did not move. Through pallid lips, he quoted in a whisper the prince's own words: 'You are a man the same as I.'

The prince faltered. He lowered his blazing eyes. Slowly, he lowered his sword arm. He turned away.

From that moment on, matters acquired their own momentum. The slaves took over the palace and much else besides. They formed their own bodies of advisers. The advisers ordered the women to weave banners, on which were embroidered such fiery slogans as ALL MEN ARE PRINCES — AND PRINCES ARE ONLY MEN. And SLAVES, FORGE YOUR SHACKLES INTO SWORDS. And SHOW YOUR STRENGTH: OVERTHROW A THRONE. Persuaded by such demonstrations, the soldiers of the royal garrison joined the slaves.

Such was the situation when the king arrived from his capital in the south with a strong army. Old he was, but warlike still, and a battle was fought within the palace grounds, to the great detriment of the flowers and livestock.

News of this civil war, as it was called, travelled fast. To the east of the kingdom lay another powerful state. Hitherto, its ruler had shown friendship to the king; but now that the king's attention was distracted, the ruler struck. With forty thousand men and two dozen elephants, he invaded the disorderly realm.

The slaves, besieged in the palace, immediately hailed the foreign invader as a liberator, and re-doubled their attacks on the king. Bravely though he and his men fought, the king's force was besieged on both sides; after one final assault, he died fighting among his soldiery. The invaders proceeded to lay waste the countryside.

The foreign ruler stepped in smartly, quartered his surviving elephants in the palace grounds, and had all the slaves paraded before him.

The southern slave, who had now given himself a smart uniform, stood forth and made a special salute he had invented.

'You are a man the same as I,' he said, uttering the now compulsory phrase of formal greeting.

'Nonsense, we'll see about that,' said the invader, and had all the ex-slaves executed.

As for the Fair Prince, he still lives in a far country, though it lies a little further away than does the country of his birth. He works in a rice field and is given two meals a day. His master is kind to him. That quality in him which nobody has named has now burned itself out and, as we said, the prince also has no name. It has been forgotten by history.

The Girl Who Sang

Mochtar Ivring peered over the flowers on his balcony and saw in the street below a beautiful girl, singing. It was the sound of her voice which had brought him to the balcony.

Most of the street lay in shadow, but the girl's head and torso were in sun. Her dark glossy hair shone, her cheeks shone. When she glanced up at him, green eyes dazzled for a moment in the early light. On her arm she carried a basket. She disappeared into a house, taking with her all the magic from the scene.

Craning to catch the last glimpse of her heel, Mochtar heard his landlady from the room behind say, 'Mind my jessikla plants, now!' He returned into his room where Mrs Bornzam was clearing his modest breakfast and making his bed.

'Beautiful singing,' he said, explaining away his supposed threat to her window-boxes.

'That's the girl who sings,' Mrs Bornzam said, with her customary air of setting in its place all that was known about the world.

The singing and the sight of the girl had momentarily lifted Mochtar's spirits, though they sank again when he contemplated the grey-clad bulk of Mrs Bornzam. The city of Matrassyl was stocked with people like Mrs Bornzam, all fat and corseted and dull and ungenerous of spirit. He had been here far too long, but was too poor to afford to leave. So he lodged with the Bornzams in the back street, and advertised in their front parlour window for pupils. At present, the number of his pupils was precisely one. The war. Everything could be blamed on the war.

Although he had all day to kill as usual, Mochtar left the house in some haste, pulling on his yellow coat as he went, buttoning up its fur collar, as he hurried into the street. Not only did he wish to avoid Mrs Bornzam's conversation which had for its *leitmotif* the contemptible inability of teachers to earn good money, but he wanted to catch another glimpse, if possible, of the girl who sang.

The street was full of Matrassylans trudging to work. They were a dumpy race with a preference for grey cloth. Mochtar raised his eyes to the distant hills, but no one else looked. When he came into a grander thoroughfare, men on horseback mingled with the crowd of pedestrians, and a cabriolet laboured slowly up to the castle, the driver lashing his horses. On the corner of this thoroughfare and the street where the Bornzams lived stood a tavern. As he paused there, the girl who sang left by one of its side doors.

The way she swung her basket told him that it was now empty, and he guessed she had been delivering bread. As she paused in the sunlight, a few notes escaped her lips. Then she saw Mochtar staring and stopped, smiling, her lips apart, to give him an enquiring look.

She was more lovely than he had imagined. Her face was rather long, though this was counterbalanced by a round little nose. Her mouth looked generous, her eyebrows were arched and a trifle severe. Heavy lashes offset her light green eyes. If these features sounded miscellaneous when catalogued, when glimpsed together their effect was delightful – even breathtaking, Mochtar thought, and before he could allow shyness to overwhelm him, he had stepped forward, raised his hat, and addressed this beautiful creature.

The beautiful creature regarded him from under her lashes. With a disarming smile, she sang a few bars of a melody and then passed by, tripping daintily up the side street. Thus a chance was presented to gaze at her slender figure, in which the dumpiness of Matrassyl was nowhere apparent.

He had certainly never heard a more delectable sound than her singing. Cloddish bodies pushed by him as he stood, striving to capture her elusive tune in his head. At one moment he thought it familiar, at the next not. The harsh sounds of Matrassyl, thrown against stone walls and cliffs and echoing back, drove it from mind.

He moved on when a squad of infantry marched noisily by, and made his way to the Question Mark. The usual one-armed beggar stood outside, but Mochtar brushed past him. He favoured this coffee house because one of the waiters was friendly, hailing from the same distant country, born within sight of the same sea, as Mochtar. After greeting his friend, he retired to his usual table and abstractedly unfurled a newspaper to see how the war was going.

War had been raging for nineteen years, prowling back and forth across the continent of Campannlat like plague, springing up again when seeming exhausted. It showed no sign of reaching any conclusion, despite the oratory of statesmen.

It was the war, and the prankish accidental nature of war, which had stranded Mochtar, at the age of twenty, in Matrassyl. Innocent of all knowledge of any such city, he was studying in a university in the Qzints, when the university town had been invaded by a Pannovalan army. The invading army took over the university buildings as its headquarters. Mochtar and other students had been made prisoner and forced to work in gangs, towing barges south-eastwards for several hundred miles along the tow-paths of the Ubingual Canal, which cut through the heart of the strife-locked continent. One stormy night, Mochtar had dodged the guard, crossed the canal, and escaped, to find himself after months of wandering in Matrassyl. He was too ill to go further. Although his strength had by now returned, return to his home by the Climent Sea was impossible; for that he needed money, and a cessation to the fighting in the western sector.

Sipping his free coffee, he scoured the blurred newsprint before him.

According to the latest report, the enemy in the west was at last in retreat, following the bitter winter campaign. The double-headed eagle had gained distinct ascendancy over the sun-and-sickle – although, in the east, in Mordriat, prospects were less bright. Somehow, the news brought Mochtar little joy, certainly not enough to dislodge the girl's tune from his head. The words ... The words of the tune ... Suddenly, he resolved a part of the puzzle. He slapped his hand on his table, rattling his cup. The girl – he should have realised as much earlier – was not singing in Olonets, the local language. She sang in Slachs, an eastern language with which Mochtar was only slightly familiar.

The friendly waiter ceased his favourite occupation of staring over the green curtain into the street, and said, mistaking Mochtar's gesture, 'The news is gratifying, yes?'

'Very gratifying. We'll be home some time, and away from this prison of a town.'

'This is the day you go to teach your lame boy?'

'Yes. He's now my only pupil, and he's a fool. Hence my failing finances.'

The waiter nodded and bent closer. 'Listen, I have a titbit for you. A fellow told me yesterday that the duke's language teacher has gone for a soldier, silly ass, to try and find his brother lost in the eastern war against the Kzaan of Mordriat.

'The duke's enlightened about foreigners, they say. Why don't you go up to the castle and try your luck?'

'I'd never dare.'

'It couldn't do any harm. Try your luck, I say, or you may be forced to take up a waiting job too. Better to teach the surly Matrassylans than serve them, I say . . . Have another cup of coffee before you leave.'

The next morning was positively springlike. When the sun Freyr rose high enough above the shoulders of the Cosgatt Mountains to shine upon the domes of the city's churches, Mochtar was already dressed and breakfasted.

Mrs Bornzam disapproved of this departure from routine as gravely as she disapproved of lateness, and expressed her displeasure by hissing through her false teeth, but her lodger escaped without delay into the street. He walked slowly up it, up to the top. It was a direction in which he rarely ventured, for the alleys became narrow and steep, and the people increasingly xenophobic. Dehorned phagors lurked in slavery here. He observed that a water-pump was being repaired. Cobbles had been taken up, a spring gushed down an adjacent way from a broken pipe, bubbling across the street.

Blessed water, he thought, which has diverted the girl who sang from her customary path towards my irresistible clutches.

As he stood where the ways met, his initiative was rewarded. Echoing among the shadowy alleys came a haunting song, and in a moment the dark girl was in sight, her basket over her arm. Her step was firm. She was as trim a vision as he had ever set eyes on.

Immediately, his hatred of the city left him. According to legend, Matrassyl had once been the capital of an empire; now it was a dull provincial town. But the beauty of the girl who sang transformed it into a miraculous place.

He raised his hat as she approached.

'May I walk with you on your way?'

She smiled with a reserve which Mochtar felt he already knew by heart. A fragment of song drifted from her red lips. Prepared for the foreign language, he thought he grasped its simple meaning: 'I care for nobody, for nobody cares for me.'

She gave no other answer. He had the benefit of her profile along most of the street. At the door of the tavern, she turned her eyes towards him and sang a few pure notes. Then she went inside.

He waited with a light heart until she emerged with a light basket. It was puzzling: the girl who sang attempted neither to evade nor to address him. Pretty and pleasant though she was, there was something withdrawn in her manner, something which made him feel it would be impertinent to return up the street with her.

'May I see you tomorrow?' he asked. He thought, if I don't see her, the sun will not shine.

When she sang, he recognised the Slachs word for 'tomorrow', but could not understand the rest of it. That vexed him, but he went on his way rejoicing in the memory of her parting smile. What a strange, what a marvellous girl . . . And not from these parts, praise be . . . Perhaps unhuman blood ran in her veins – the blood of the Madis, let's say. Before he knew it, he had climbed the hill and was at the Anganol Gate of the castle.

The dukes of Matrassyl had seen grand times, but misfortunes of war had reduced their pomp. Mochtar was shown into a room with an unlit stove where the curtains, funereal at long windows, had moth holes in them. He sat on a side-chair, contemplating a portrait of the emperor, above which hung a tattered flag bearing the double-headed eagle, the bird of Oldorando-Borlien. Clutching his hat, he thought how the world was loaded against the young; even the expression about the emperor's whiskers proclaimed as much. You had to fight back as best you could.

When a withered clerk entered the room, Mochtar stood up. The clerk asked him a few questions. After another wait, he was shown into the presence of the duke.

The duke sat at a polished table. He wore a green velvet jacket with lace cuffs. And a wig. Apart from a large ruby ring on one finger, and a melancholy expression, he appeared much like any ordinary human being in middle life. Unsmilingly, he motioned Mochtar to sit on the opposite side of the table, so that they could both study the other's reflection in the polished table-top.

'I have three children. I wish them to be taught Ponpt, which I understand is your native language, to a standard where they can speak it fluently and read its great works of religious literature with ease.'

'Yes, your grace.'

'The times are ill, M. Ivring, and will remain so until the forces of the sun-and-sickle are defeated. Because of the confounded war, I wish also to have my children coached in the barbarous eastern tongue of Slachdom. You have no command of Slachs, I assume?'

Caught between a wish to be honest and a wish to secure the job, Mochtar paused. Then, rather to his own surprise, he sang in his light tenor voice, in Slachs, 'I care for nobody, for nobody cares for me.'

The duke was impressed. He screwed a monocle into his left eye and surveyed Mochtar carefully.

'You are engaged, sir. My clerk will furnish you with details of salary and so forth. Before you go, outline for me your philosophy of life.'

In the midst of the paralysis which this question induced, Mochtar thought that very likely dukes were trained to freeze the air about them; it went with their exalted station in life. He recalled his pleasant home-city by the western sea, where the gulls cried; he thought of the desolate plains and mountains within which Matrassyl was ensconced; he thought of the yet more desolate lands to the east, the lands which led ultimately to the High Nktryhk, from whence, mysteriously, a girl who sang had come, emerging from clouds of war. And he thought of saying to the duke, There is no philosophy, only geography; Helliconia is a function, and humanity a part of that function. But that might not meet the case at all.

'I believe in rationality, your grace. That people should conduct their lives without superstition . . . '

'It sounds commendable enough. How do you define superstition?'

'Well, your grace, we should trust to the evidence of the intellect. I can believe in this table because I can see it; yesterday, if challenged on the point, I would have been within my rights not to have believed in it, because my senses had not informed me of its existence. Hearsay evidence would not have been sufficient.'

The duke's hand went to an elaborate inkstand and played with it, seemingly without permission from the duke, who sat stiffly upright.

'You chose a trivial example upon which to suppose yourself questioned. Let us say the interrogation concerned not a piece of furniture but

Almighty Akhanaba, who elects not to show himself to us. What then?'

'From this day on, I shall believe in your table, your grace, because I have witnessed its existence, and could if necessary give some account of it.'

The duke rose and pulled the bell-cord. 'Be sure you teach your charges your language and literature, not your philosophy. I am also a rationalist – but one evidently of larger capacity than you. I believe in this table as evidence of God Almighty as well as mere evidence of itself. As I see my reflection in it, so I see His.'

'Yes, your grace.'

As the dry clerk returned to escort Mochtar out, the duke said, 'Undiluted rationality leads to death of the spirit. You sing. Remember that songs are frequently to be trusted above prose, and metaphor above so-called reality.'

From that day on, Mochtar's affairs prospered. He saw more of the girl who sang – and not only in the mornings but in the evenings and on her free afternoons. He put one or two rivals to flight. Discovering more about her became one with the advance of spring, which grew greener every day although Helliconia was entering the autumn of another Great Year. They walked in the daisy-starred meadows above the grey town, and she sang, 'Love is all lies and deception, And my lover hides in the dark wild wood.'

They sat on a fallen tree trunk, looking down at the city below, where little dumpy people moved in miniature streets. Beyond the town flowed the river, the chill Takissa. Above them, the steep meadows gave way to the harsher slopes of the Cosgatt. Somewhere up there, so rumour had it, an army flying the banners of the sun-and-sickle was approaching Matrassyl. The girl hugged her knees and sang about a house

97

untended, where women's hearts were empty because their men were off to fight at a place called Kalitka.

Beyond the city walls, the life of the country reasserted itself. Fish flashed in the river, and a heron waited immobile for them on the bank. Butterflies and bees were at work in the scantiom nearby. Beetles glinted in the tall grass. Both suns shone. Everywhere lay double shadows, double highlights. He gestured contemptuously at the city which distance had diminished. 'Look at it – you could put it in your pocket, castle and all.'

But she had no answer for him, only her touching lament.

'Never mind Kalitka,' he said. 'What about Matrassyl and you and me? What about those highly important topics, eh?'

He grasped her impatiently, but she shook free and jumped to her feet. She looked blank, and the song died on her lips. Standing with her mouth slightly open, she presented a picture of maimed beauty.

One evening in her doorway, he kissed her lips. She put an arm about his neck and softly sang, 'Don't drive the horses too hard, coachman. There's still a long, long way to go.'

Together with the spring and their developing relationship went Mochtar's increasing involvement with the two sons and the daughter of the duke. Their ages were five, six, and eight. Though they were haughty with their language tutor, they attended to his lessons, and made steady progress in Ponpt.

Sometimes, the duchess, a thin lady in velvets, arrived at the door of the schoolroom, and listened without speaking. Sometimes the duke would appear, cramming his bulk into a small desk to attend, frowning, to what Mochtar had to say. This embarrassed his employee, all too aware of his scanty knowledge of Slachs.

Sombre though the duke's demeanour was, Mochtar detected an errant spirit under the surface; whereas her grace appeared to possess no character at all, beyond a stifled way of breathing.

'M. Ivring,' said the duke, drawing him aside on one occasion, 'you may apply to the librarian, with my permission, to refer to my books. You will find there a section of volumes on Slachdom, including – if memory serves – a grammar of the Slachs tongue.'

Not since he had been forced to leave his university studies had Mochtar seen as many volumes as the library contained. The section printed in Slachs was particularly precious. It drew him nearer to the girl who sang. Here he could study her language, and make out something of the history of her race.

One afternoon, when he was sunk deep in a leather chair, reading, the duke appeared and screwed his monocle into his eye.

'You are deriving benefit from the library, my rationalist friend?'

'Yes, your grace.' Mochtar realised that this stiff-backed man, the Duke of Matrassyl – not ancient, perhaps no more ancient than twenty-eight years old, though that was ancient enough – was attempting to be friendly. Beyond closing his volume with a finger in it, Mochtar made no move to respond.

'You probably wonder how I came to have such a collection of volumes relating to Slachdom.'

Having wondered nothing of the sort, Mochtar kept silent.

The duke walked about before saying, 'I led a campaign to the east, very successfully. We put the forces of the Kzaan of Mordriat to flight. A great victory, a great victory. That was ten years ago. Unfortunately, it did not end the war, and now the enemy has gathered strength again, and isn't too far from here ... ' He sighed heavily.

'Anyhow, we plundered one of the strongholds of the Kzaan, and these books were part of the booty. They're decently bound, I'll give the barbarian that.'

He swung about on his heel in a military way, leaving as abruptly as he had come. Dismissing him from mind, Mochtar returned to his history of the Slachi.

The Slachi were a nation within a nation. They lived chiefly in the mountain ranges of the vast country of Mordriat, often as shepherds or brigands. They were persecuted from time to time. Many of the men were forced through poverty to join the Mordriat Kzaan's armies, where they served the sun-and-sickle loyally. Indeed, their prowess in war had enabled some exceptional Slachi to become Kzaans. Despite such occasional glories, the history of their race was one of misfortune. There had once been an independent Slachi nation, but it was overwhelmed at the battle of Kalitka ('still a subject for epic poetry', said the chronicle), six centuries previously.

As Mochtar's friendship with the girl who sang grew, so grew his knowledge of her ethnic background, and of her language.

So also did her mystery grow. She never spoke. She could not speak. She could only sing her songs. Though people in the back streets of Matrassyl knew her because of her singing, no one was her friend. None could say her name. She was the eternal foreigner.

The girl who sang worked in a bakery and lived in a garret. She had no parents, no relations, no one near her who spoke Slachs. She had no possessions, as far as Mochtar could discover – except for a long-necked binnaduria inlaid with mother-of-pearl, with which she sometimes accompanied her songs.

So beautiful was her singing that the birds of garden and meadow ceased their own warbling to listen. They would gather about her high window as they never did about the casements of those who threw them grain.

'I'm a foreigner in this town, as you are, my darling. Where were you born? Do you remember?'

'The walls of Lestanávera stand high above the stream. But life in Lestanávera is nothing but a dream,' she sang in her own tongue.

'Is that your home, Lestanávera?'

'Alas, the traitorous Vuk at night who opened the gate, Betrayed old Lestanávera and Slachi fate.'

'Were you there then, my poor love?'

She could not reply, unless her lingering regard was a reply.

In the duke's library after lessons the next day, Mochtar found a reference to Lestanávera. It had been a great fortress on the Madavera, the main river of the vanquished kingdom of Slachi. A traitor named Vuk Sudar had opened the gate to the Mordriat enemy and the impregnable fortress fell. Two years later came the fateful battle of Kalitka, when the Slachi nation was finally defeated, its leaders and soldiers slain.

In so many of her songs, Mochtar reflected as he walked back to his room, she made reference to events long bygone. The realisation came to him slowly that not only was song her sole means of communication: her songs were traditional, referring to events long past. The shadowy power of Lestanávera, a place he had had to look up in a book, might be either the power natural to her birthplace, or to a legend born long before her grandparents' time.

'Late again, and me standing over the pot for you,' Mrs Bornzam said, when he entered his lodgings. Mochtar took his evening meal with the senior Bornzams and their two loutish sons – a doubtful privilege. Since he was late, and politely brought up, he apologised.

'I should think so,' the lady said, in a tone implying that she found his apologies as irritating as his unpunctuality. 'Just because you work for the duke, you needn't ape the manners of the duke.'

He let his anger simmer throughout the meal, eating little despite the blandishments of old Bornzam, who was a civil enough fellow, considering that he worked in the town abattoir. He waited until after the meal, when Mrs Bornzam stacked all the dirty plates and cutlery into her sink, added her pair of china false teeth to the pile, and began the washing-up. Her teeth were always done with the dishes, and dried afterwards on the same towel, before being reinserted in her mouth.

Mochtar worked himself up to deliver something cruel, but managed only to say, 'Mrs Bornzam, I shall be leaving this house tomorrow. I will pay you till the end of the month. I refuse to eat at your table again.'

She looked round at him in horror, her cheeks turning a dull red. Fishing in the washing-up water with one hand, she brought her teeth up dripping, and pushed them into her mouth to say, 'And what's so wrong with my table, then, you little scholarly prig? You won't get better meat at any other table that's sure.'

'It's not at all sure. It's a very debatable statement. Mrs Bornzam, your temper might be better if you sang everything you had to say. You might then be less intolerable.'

'You cheeky little pipsqueak!'

'Though doubtless if you attempted to sing, your teeth would fall out. Good night, madam.'

Feeling less triumphant next morning, Mochtar told his troubles to the girl who sang.

'Hide away your tear, Only the binnaduria sounds sweet all year long.'

He kissed her passionately. 'Why can you not speak, you beauty? Yet how I love your voice. What has happened to you that the ordinary power of words has deserted you?'

What with the practice that she and his pupils gave him, he now spoke easily to her in her native tongue.

'Only the binnaduria sounds sweet all year long.'

'It's not true. You also sound sweet – always.'

That word 'always' lingered in his mind as he climbed the road to the castle. To have her for always ... To take her away from grey Matrassyl, away to the sea ... But his daydreams shattered as ever on the rational rock of his having too little money. He had received a letter from his father – it had been on its way for months – but it enclosed no money for him. Damn his father, the old rogue.

Fortune, however, still smiled on him. At the close of the morning's lesson, the duke entered the schoolroom. He had a widowed cousin who also wished to learn Slachs. Would M. Ivring be her tutor for a salary she and he could agree between themselves? They expected the lady at the castle on the following day.

Mochtar had had to give up his lame pupil, the son of a burgher, in order to teach at the castle. With four pupils, his salary should be sufficient to get married on, if he could find a good room locally.

The dream changed. He would live for ever in Matrassyl with the girl who sang, and she would slowly come to speak prose like everyone else.

That evening at Freyrset he asked her to marry him. He thought she accepted him. She sang that all the girls of the village admired the handsome young shepherd, but he had eyes for only one of the girls. She sang of a handkerchief that gleamed in the moonlight by a ruin where two young lovers had met. She sang that the river Madavera flowed by a cottage, where all who passed in boats heard a young girl singing to express her happiness. She sang, she played her bin-naduria, she danced for him, she wept. It seemed like an acceptance.

There was no difficulty in finding a pleasant but rather expensive room in which to set up house. They consoled themselves for their extravagance by admiring the beautiful view of the river. The girl who sang knew many songs about rivers. Rivers, with ruins, broken wine glasses, soldiers, deserted lovers, lost letters, and old mothers, formed a large part of her repertoire.

The wedding ceremony presented difficulties, but Mochtar, aided by his waiter friend, found an under-standing priest who agreed to join them in matrimony.

'I knew a nun with the same affliction,' the man of God observed. 'She had been raped by an enemy soldier, or perhaps it was a friendly one, and never after uttered another word. Except for her devotional singing, which was much valued in the nunnery.'

So Mochtar and the girl who sang were married, and returned in happiness to their room with a view. The bride clutched her groom, kissed him, and sang sweetly, but evaded all the usual pleasant intimacies of the bed.

It was therefore a rather gloomy Mochtar who returned to the castle to meet his new pupil. The Lady Ljubima was not the gaunt old figure in black his imagination had painted. She was a fair-haired woman of his own age, brightly dressed and flirtatious of manner. Even the duke looked more cheerful in her presence. She informed Mochtar immediately that she liked him and had no intention of mourning an old husband who had been foolish enough to get himself killed on a silly battlefield.

Standing like a statue to integrity, Mochtar informed her that while he was prepared to teach her a foreign language, he felt bound to tell her that he was newly married. She laughed, not at all put out, and named a generous sum she was prepared to pay as long as the lessons were not too dull.

Despite himself, he found himself growing to like Ljubima. She had wit, and she detested Matrassyl as cordially as he. She treated him as a slightly dim equal, and told him amusing stories of life in what she termed her 'tin-pot palace', now overrun by the hated sun-and-sickle. Their friendship progressed faster than their lessons.

When Mochtar returned to his room, there was his lovely wife, to sing to him and kiss him and cook him gorgeous meals – but not to grant him the intimacies he craved. Every day he discovered how expensive meat was, and how dusty repressed desire.

'What ails you, my love?' he asked her tenderly – he was tender to her at this time. 'What has befallen you?'

She took up her long-necked binnaduria and sang him a heartbreaking song of a lass who walked late in her garden one night, and none thereafter knew why she pined away, pined away.

He took to writing down the words of her songs that summer. She gladly helped him, singing each phrase over, her hand resting on his shoulder. At first, he did it for love, without mercenary intention. Growing more ambitious, he took music lessons in the evening with an old crone in the lower town, in order to be able to transcribe the notes of her songs into his book.

As he was walking home one evening late, Mochtar was hailed from a hansom cab. It was his fair pupil, the Lady Ljubima. She offered to drive him home, and he climbed up beside her. But she called to her driver, and they clip-clopped to her house at a great rate.

105

'For a glass of wine, no more!' she cried, laughing at his concern. 'Don't think I'm offering you anything else, little scholar.'

'I don't doubt that!' he said, suddenly bitter. 'Women like to lead men on – only to deny them the one thing they want.'

'Oh, la! And will you name that one thing?'

'You know what I mean – the rational end of desire.'

More sympathetically, she said, 'You speak with experience.'

'With *in*experience, more like.'

When they reached the mansion, Ljubima said she was tired, she dismissed the servants and took him into her boudoir, where she poured him a glass of spiced wine. They sat companionably on a chaise longue, and Mochtar found himself pouring out the story of his strange wife. At first, he felt ashamed of his loose tongue, but a passion for declaration soon overcame him.

Silence fell when he finished.

A tear stole down Ljubima's cheek. 'Mochtar, dear Mochtar, thank you for confiding in me. Your wife sounds such a rare person. No doubt she underwent some terrible experience as a young girl – that's a tragedy. But it is obvious how much she loves and trusts you. No doubt in a year or two she will feel confident enough to grant you all you desire and more.'

'A year! A year or two! You think I can wait so long?'

She tried to calm him. He seized more wine and drank it down, flinging the glass on to the rug, where it lay without shattering.

'You must wait. Oh, yours is such a rare love! I will never do anything to sully it. Forgive me! – I admit that, on a whim, because you're amusing, I did play with the idea of a seduction scene, this being a night I am free, but now – '

He turned furiously on her.

106

'Played with the idea – played with me, you mean! Just as she does. A rare love! Rare indeed! Take your clothes off, you bitch, or I swear I'll kill you.'

'I'll call the servants and have you shot. One scream is all it needs.'

He stood back. 'Ljubima, forgive me, I'm not rational. Let me stay with you tonight, I beg. I will offer no violence, only love. I'm not a violent man. Please, if you find I'm acceptable, amuse yourself as you intended. For myself, you know how I have grown fond of you.'

She sat. Then she raised her hands and began to unpin her hair.

'Are you sure this is what you most want?'

'Oh, yes, yes, darling Ljubima!' He fell on his knees, seizing one of her hands and kissing it. 'How can you be so sweet to me, a commoner?'

'Ask nothing – just accept,' she said. 'And don't flatter yourself by thinking of me as nobility. I'm just a woman overtaken by war.'

He did not pause to puzzle out her remark.

The girl who sang did not reproach her husband when he appeared late next day. Instead, she gave voice to a slow song of intricate rhythm, to which the refrain was, 'Oh, Marick, Marick, are you dead, As in my dreams you were?' Smiling, she executed a gentle dance before him. He covered his eyes.

During the next afternoon lesson, Mochtar and Ljubima were formal. At the end of it, as they rose from the schoolroom table, she said in a low voice, 'I accepted you last night because of the touching story of your marriage, nothing more.'

'That is not what you said then. When may I come and see you again?'

She looked down at the worn carpet. 'The war

from the east draws nearer Matrassyl, day by day. Who knows what will become of us all?'

He thought that her words could have been set to music.

As she left the room, she said casually, 'You could come tomorrow night. I'll be free then. My cab will pick you up at the Old Square.'

Because she seemed so wealthy and he so poor, he thought, I'm really lucky, but everything would be better if only I had more money.

The next time the Duke of Matrassyl entered the classroom to observe the progress his children were making, Mochtar ventured to address him.

'Your grace, your children are both brilliant and diligent at their studies. However, they lack mastery of the correct Slachs accent, that all-important matter, which I, not being of Slachi origin, am unable to impart in all its nuances. May I make so bold as to suggest that I hire for you a lady I have encountered, a Slachi, who could come to the castle and enunciate for your children and your Lady cousin, to their decided advantage?'

The duke regarded him from under his iron eyebrows.

'When you were first engaged, young man, my impression was that you had little Slachs, though I grant you progressed rapidly. Supposing this lady you have encountered . . . proves herself a better teacher than you. Will you not then have engineered yourself out of a job?'

'This lady, your grace, speaks only her own language. She will be a perfect example but an imperfect teacher, you'll find.'

'You are still a rationalist, I perceive. Very well, bring her along.'

'She is much in demand, your grace, and not only comes somewhat expensive, but requests strongly

108

that your grace pay her through me before she appears.'

The duke took a long look out of the window towards the mountains.

'Well, the enemy may be at the Takissa before the autumn. Before that fate befalls us, we must all enjoy life as much as we can.'

He sighed heavily. 'I have reason to believe that our old enemy, the Kzaan, will raze Matrassyl to the ground if he gets here . . . ' And he paid Mochtar the amount he demanded.

When Mochtar arrived home, he explained to his wife that she would have to sing at the castle the next day. 'Sing and dance, that will be best. We must earn some money. When the enemy gets near the gates, we are going to escape, and that requires resources. My friend in the Question Mark will come with us. Three will travel safer than two.'

Her breasts heaved beneath her blouse, and she began to sing quietly of Lestanávera, now only a ruin, where once many a handsome man and maid were seen.

'Never mind Lestanávera, my dear, let's eat supper fast, because I have to go out this evening.'

Over the pot on the stove, she hummed quietly to herself. It was the song, he recognised, about a girl who looked after her father's swine; she called to them and the swine heard her voice; but the one whom she longed to hear was dead beneath the winter's snow. He checked to make sure it was in his collection.

By now, he had over two hundred Slachs folk songs, many of them several centuries old. In the civilised capitals of the West, the collection would be worth a great deal, and his name would be made when they were published.

There was great activity as Mochtar made his way to the castle with his wife. Soldiers were marching through the streets, and a band was playing. As the band stopped, Mochtar understood the reason for the excitement. Distant cannonfire boomed in the hills. The forces of the sun-and-sickle were nearing the Takissa. He said nothing to his wife.

She sang a repertoire of songs to her audience of four, just as Mochtar demanded. To his disappointment, the duke and duchess did not appear. As they were about to leave the castle, however, the duke was standing in the hall talking to two army officers. He also was in uniform, with sword and pistol at his belt, looking formidable. A line of armed phagor guards waited motionless behind him. When he saw Mochtar, he called him over. The duke's manner was curt, his expression grim.

'I may be absent for some while. You are dismissed, Ivring. Draw what salary is owed you – my clerk will see to it – and don't come here again, ever.'

Mochtar was dumbfounded.

'But why, your grace – '

'You're dismissed, I said. Go.'

'But I must say goodbye to Lady – '

The duke, in turning a uniformed shoulder on him, noticed the girl who sang for the first time, and beckoned her to him. He said something to the generals, who immediately became interested.

She approached, and eyed the duke with an open curiosity in which her usual innocence protected her from fear.

'What's your name, my dark-haired beauty?'

She sang a few pure notes, 'My name is sorrow, I'm from Distack.' It was No 82 in Mochtar's book.

One of two officers immediately took the girl by her arm, while the other officer drove Mochtar away.

110

'I never argue with an armed man,' he said, and fled, ignoring his wife's cries.

When he collected his fee from the duke's clerk, who would tell him nothing, he hurried from the castle. Pushing through the crowded streets, he went to cheer himself up at the Question Mark, where he gave an account of the duke's behaviour to his friend, the waiter.

'I can't understand it,' he said. 'I was the perfect teacher.'

'The war's coming this way,' said the waiter. 'Faster than expected. You're a foreigner, aren't you? Well, that's the way they treat foreigners in this rotten town. I should know.'

'Yes, you must be right. Then why did they seize my wife?'

The waiter spread his hands. It was all so obvious to him. 'Why, she's a foreigner, too, isn't she? What else can you expect in a place like Matrassyl?'

'I suppose you're right. Get me a bottle of wine, will you? What a mean way to behave to an honest chap . . . '

He spent several hours drinking in the coffee house and studying the newspaper, which was full of bad news from East and West. The only item to offer encouragement was an obscure paragraph on a back page, which announced the death of a composer in his home country. Someone would have to take his place. Composers were always needed, in war as in peace. He would have to see about arranging the songs, to make them more palatable to a cultured public.

Going heavily home, he was surprised to find his room empty. His wife had not yet returned. Who would prepare his supper? Why, their bed was not even made, curse her.

Suddenly, he was angry. What pleasure had he

ever enjoyed on that bed? She gave him nothing, never would. But there were others . . .

His mind dwelt luxuriously on Lady Ljubima, on her beauty and ardour. Also on her way with words, always so precise, always saying exactly what she intended. A rational person, like him. Really – one had to admit it – being married to someone who could not talk or make love was misery.

He took a drink from a brandy bottle, tramping round the room, and came suddenly to a decision.

Pulling his old pack from under the bed, he stuffed some essentials into it. The bottle went in. So did the priceless folk song collection. At the door, he paused and looked round. Her long-necked binnaduria lay on the dresser. Yes, it would serve her right if he took it. At least he'd get something from her. He grabbed it.

As he walked through the streets of Matrassyl for the last time, he saw his future clear. He would be doing Ljubima a favour. He was rescuing her from certain death. Rape. Torture. All the rest of it. This was one of the evenings she had forbidden him to see her – but what of that? Her cab was what he needed. They would escape in the cab. She would have valuables. They'd drive westward, never stopping. Never stopping till they reached the western sea. There they would live happily and prosperously, and he would be famous.

It was a long way on foot to her mansion. Double darkness had fallen by the time he arrived. As he passed under the light by the gate, he saw her holding a candle at an upper window. Ljubima saw Mochtar and waved frantically.

'She's crazy for me,' he told himself, smiling.

Her footman opened the door. He stepped into the hall. The duke of Matrassyl emerged from Ljubima's parlour. His monocle was in his left eye. He levelled a double-barrelled pistol at Mochtar. He trembled with suppressed fury.

This apparition so astonished Mochtar that his legs began immediately to quake. He could hardly stand up, never mind speak.

'I'm glad to see you so dismayed,' said the duke, speaking in a thick voice. 'You have earned yourself a reputation as rather a cool customer. I discover you have had the infernal temerity to visit my mistress here, in the very house in which I have installed her. She has told me everything, so don't deny it.'

'But, but she − '

'You are going to be shot. I am going to shoot you. Say nothing. Pray to Akhanaba.'

Mochtar's knees collapsed. He fell sobbing to the marble tiles.

'But my poor wife ... '

'A little late to think of her.' The duke had a grim smile on his face, as if he was enjoying these moments considerably more than Mochtar. 'Ten years ago, when fighting in the eastern campaign, one of my generals took an enemy position, and we found we had captured the family of the Great Kzaan of Mordriat − the Kzaan having fled in true Slachi fashion. My men put all the family to the bayonet, except for the Kzaan's wife and daughter, the latter scarcely seven years old. They were seized for ransom. That was a lucky day for us.'

Mochtar looked up supplicatingly, but the duke kicked him back into a crouching position.

'Both the mother and the daughter were raped on their way back here, and unfortunately the Kzaanina died. The daughter escaped from us one night. We assumed she had either died or found her way back to Mordriat. But no. You, my resourceful little trickster, found her in the back streets of this very city. Her mind's gone, but she's still of great value. The Kzaan

113

will spare Matrassyl in order to get his daughter back alive.'

Through his snivels, Mochtar had been listening hard. He rose to his knees now, to say, 'Your grace, please believe me, I was about to hand her over. That was why I brought her to the castle, don't you see? You can't shoot the saviour of Matrassyl.'

A pleasant laugh sounded behind the duke.

'You can't shoot him, Advard. Let him go. He means no real harm — unlike the Kzaan, with whom you are prepared to deal. I wish more of the soldiers had Mochtar's nerve.'

The duke turned scowling to where Ljubima stood, tall and fair, holding before her a candle in a golden candlestick.

'You love this crawling commoner,' he said, raising the pistol.

'Oh no, no, Advard. On the contrary. He almost raped me. I'd be glad to see him go. But I hate to see people being killed.'

Mollified by this response, the duke turned back to Mochtar. This time, something sheepish had entered into his manner.

'Listen, I shall count to ten, boy, and then I shall shoot you if you are still here. One.'

Mochtar was through the door by Three.

By Five he was back.

He smiled nervously at the duke and Ljubima.

'Sorry. I forgot my pack and my binnaduria.'

He grabbed them and ran for the door.

'Nine. Ten.'

Both barrels of the pistol fired. But Mochtar had fled into the night.

The Plain,
the Endless Plain

The forest, which had been growing slowly more impenetrable, ended without warning.

Relieved to escape from the trees, the Tribe emerged one by one and grouped together to stand gazing at the territory which confronted them. Ahead stretched an almost featureless plain.

In their weariness, they did not communicate. No statement was needed to convey the starkness of their situation.

The plain which stretched before them was so immense and nondescript that it existed almost as an abstraction. Its indeterminate area presented itself as little more than a texture under the drab sky. Nothing moved on it. Such contours as the plain possessed were lost in its colossal scale. Such colours as it possessed were also lost, submerged in a prevailing tawniness. Over all of its expanse, no hill or tree or monument broke its supine geography; so that despite its magnitude it did not transcend the petty, as if it were there only to be sucked at and finally devoured by the hazes of distance.

In all the expanse there was no sign of welcome for the Tribe, no refuge. They stood there in a group,

115

appalled, bludgeoned by the dimensions stretching before them.

Behind them, however, the Enemy still advanced through the green intestines of the jungle, moving confidently, without caution, as the noise as from a steel foundry testified. To survive, it was necessary for the Tribe to venture out into the wilderness, hoping that the enemy would not follow but instead turn back into the fastnesses from which it had emerged.

A consultation was held, in which all members of the Tribe joined. They could not agree to press forward on to the plain. They had not determination enough. Some argued that they should skirt the jungle and hope to discover a river or safer place where they could take refuge.

Only when, among the thickets to their rear, the heavy metallic noise of enemy pursuit, coupled with the macabre wail of an electronic bugle, persuaded them that haste was required of them, did they understand that they must retreat into the plain or perish. The Enemy advanced on too broad a front for any other manoeuvre to be feasible.

At this time, the Tribe numbered only twenty-one. Some of them still remembered the time when their peaceful existence in the hills had been shattered. The arrival of the Enemy had been sudden and remorseless.

Goaded into haste, despite their weariness, they moved forward. The Tribe had no banners as did the Enemy. Their progress was humble, their movements dogged. They walked close in a single file, keeping always to a strict order.

They soon became engulfed within the great volume of the plain.

The first time they stopped to rest, they could look back and see the forest, an irresolute strip of blue-green behind them. At the time of their second rest, distance had dissolved the sight. They were absolutely alone in the annihilating marches which the plain represented.

Courage – or a kind of dumb continuance – was a distinct feature of the Tribe's group characteristics. Each supported the other. Nobody spoke of turning back. Their sense of direction was good. They proceeded forward without hesitation, travelling westward. Day followed day.

These were the twenty-one referred to later as Generation One.

As they became more familiar with the plain, they found that its monotony was broken by features not apparent to anyone viewing it from a distance. There were lines of low hills, rather like the ripples in a quilt, which formed obstacles to their progress. Colour, though muted, was abundant: the plain was no desert, and supported mysterious lines of low vegetation of various hues, purple, green, brown. The general colour of the land was sepia, or oatmeal.

No rain fell, yet there were winds which were no more than whispers, bringing a spray of moisture. More frequently, clouds of dust blew in their faces. The prevailing weather was tepid, without force.

The Enemy followed them. The dull glint of its armour could be seen when its extended lines crossed the low hills. Its clangour could be heard. The Tribe remained constantly alert, never resting for long, never sleeping for long, pressing ever forward into the heart of the plain.

Only at one time did they halt, for any considerable period, when it was the time to reproduce. Many progeny were born to them. As soon as the young were strong enough, the march forward was resumed. The pace increased, watch after watch, in order to draw further ahead of the pursuit.

The field of their vision was circumscribed. The light

was constant but dim. All that could be determined in the sky overhead was a whitish haze. When the Tribe came to a line of hills, they would stand there on each others' shoulders and stare ahead. Never were they rewarded with the sight of anything that promised change. All that existed was the plain, the endless plain – and the senseless pursuit.

Generation One became old and died one by one, but within a short space of each other. Their deserted husks were left behind as quickly fading landmarks. Generation Two continued as their parents had done, and begat a further generation. Generation Three numbered three hundred and two thousand, four hundred individuals, the number divided equally among the seven *septs*.

Like the previous generation, Generation Three progressed ever forward across the plain, walking in parallel single files. The Enemy continued to pursue, its menacing blades sometimes lost in the prevailing haze, sometimes appearing dramatically near, its cruel noise intensified. Food was always available. The terrain underfoot was of a curious texture, stiff yet yielding. The Tribe walked, in fact, over the tops of a stiff, dense, shrub-like vegetation. The vegetation turned dry small leaves to the air and conserved moisture at its roots, where darkness prevailed. Down there in the darkness lived lumbering cretaceans the Tribe called Arntrods.

The Arntrods were numerous and easy to hunt. The hunters of the Tribe pushed their way down through the stiff foliage to where, among the stems, there was room to crawl. Here herds of pallid Arntrods browsed. They could not elude the hunters. In no time, they were speared and their twitching bodies passed up to the surface.

At feeding time, the grey Arntrod carapaces could be cracked as easily as the shells of eggs. The flesh inside was of a lumpy texture, like scrambled egg, and almost tasteless.

Harmless though the Arntrods were, they sheltered a small parasitic creature called a Toid, which the Tribe feared. The Toids, tiny, ginger, nimble, ran everywhere, their feet stinging all they touched. They worked their way into the joints of the Tribe, causing intense pain and sometimes death. The progress of the Tribe across the plain was often halted when they were forced to disinfest each other of the hated Toids.

Despite casualties, the generation managed to reproduce itself. The *septs* gathered in traditional fashion, six bodies interlocking, matching sides, with the mother locked inside the sexagonal, penetrated from all angles simultaneously. Out from her ruined body spurted the ova, some of the young hatching while still in the air. Generation Four numbered over thirty-six million, two hundred and eighty thousand. As undaunted as their predecessors, they continued across the expanses of the plain, moving ever westwards.

Generation Four, progressing in long parallel files through the wilderness, was beset with rumours and speculations. In particular they discussed the nature of Generation One, what had been its objectives, its characteristics. Had the twenty-one members of Generation One known where the plain would end? Had they an intuition of how many generations were needed to cross it? Did they know what lay on the other side of the plain? Rumours abounded of a beautiful land, where rain fell and sun shone and there were no Toids.

More pessimistic stories described how much knowledge had been lost, generation by generation. Some claimed that Generation One were giants who had conceived a great Plan now unfolding, unbeknown to the present generation. One day soon, it was whispered, the Twenty-one would reappear, reincarnated, and lead the present generation to a better land, where they would not have to travel and food would be plentiful.

But it was not until Generation Five, which numbered over four billion, that such speculations gave way to action. Generation Five became sure of its strength, and resolved that a stand must be made against the Enemy. It refused to retreat further as its predecessors had done.

A range of hills, slightly higher than others which had been traversed, came into view. Generation Five climbed to the long crest and arrayed itself along the crest in battle order. It turned to await the approach of the Enemy.

So poor was the general visibility that it was hard to determine the strength of the Enemy. As it approached with its horrible machine-noise, with that thudding clangour as characteristic as a scent, its metallic banners could be seen to spread across the horizon from one side to the other. Yet the Tribe kept their formation.

The Enemy's rate of advance slowed. Now the Tribe could discern both the huge units and the small which comprised the force. Some of its battle-towers were the size of large mobile pyramids.

Fear struck the Tribe. But all individuals held their ground without panic. Saboteurs were sent out, who progressed along the true ground, close to the roots of the vegetation where the Arntrods grazed. The saboteurs were able to move unseen as far as the enemy engines, destroying their tracks and feelers.

Slower and slower went the Enemy's foremost wave. It ground to a halt. The two forces confronted each other. Nobody moved. Food became scarce as day succeeded day.

The Tribe grew anxious. They dared not attack, so

formidable did the Enemy appear. On the other hand, they were loath to resume a progress which would now seem more than ever like a retreat. A further dilemma was that the time for reproduction approached; at that period they would be most vulnerable to an aggressive move, and could easily be overwhelmed by a remorseless foe.

In the end, it was starvation which drove them back into the level plain. The Tribe had no idea whether the Enemy needed to eat or whether it drew its nourishment from radiations in the air. They knew only that they were beginning themselves to die, to wither inside their carapaces. Leaving a line of dead husks still to face the Enemy, the surviving members of Generation Five crept down the far side of the hill and resumed their progress towards the west.

The generations passed. Each generation travelled across the endless wastes, multiplied itself, and perished. Generation Six was the lost generation, striving to repair the damage done to morale by the previous generation. Generation Seven suffered immoderately, since they came upon a region which was increasingly desert. The stiff vegetation was eroded, the Arntrods disappeared. There was nothing for it but to progress relentlessly, leaving the dead and dying behind.

But the desert dwindled, giving way to a territory marked by brighter colours which dyed the landscape with complex patterns. Some of the patterns were traversed only when many days had passed, but there were those who suggested that they represented diagrams of living things, drawn on the surface of the plain on a gigantic scale. It was Generation Eight which was christened the Parrot Generation.

Generation Eight, in traversing the plain, made two discoveries. In the first place, they discovered that they were no longer being pursued by the Enemy. The Enemy had gone. There was no Enemy any longer.

Perhaps the Enemy had been deterred by the barrier of the dead bodies of Generation Five. Whatever the reason, it became apparent that pursuit was no more. Generation Eight, now numbering itself in trillions, was shocked into immobility. One of the chief motivations of the Tribe had suddenly been erased. Nobody knew how long it was since the Enemy had withdrawn; all they could say was that the conditions of life were altered.

The Tribe was unable to advance further. They spread over the plain in all directions, aimlessly looking for sustenance, but not progressing. So they happened on the Parrot, as it became known.

The elders among the Tribe had been studying the strange patterns of the landscape, hoping to discover there some hint as to which way they could best advance. Permanent watch was kept on the sky, in case the gigantic and presumably supernatural beings who had inscribed the landscape on such a gigantic scale should return. Word spread among them that the Tribe was now covering an area on which had been emblazoned the likeness of one of the parrots which, folk-memory insisted, once haunted the forests from which the Twenty-One had emerged.

At last a sign had been given to the marching generations. Amid great excitement, the Tribe assembled itself along the outlines of the supposed Parrot. Hunger was forgotten in a great surge of optimism that they were at last to be released from their travails.

When the outlines of the Parrot were covered by individuals, one wing of the Tribe could not see the other. Those who stood on the supposed beak could see no further than those who stood on the supposed feathers of the stomach. Nevertheless, the speedy scouts who were despatched to circumnavigate the figure returned to report excitedly that the configuration definitely conformed to the popular conception of the designated bird.

The elders now proclaimed that the gift of flight was about to be bestowed upon the Tribe. The next generation, Generation Nine, would be able to fly, and would then lead the rest from the accursed plain. Everyone sat back to await the time of reproduction with positive determination to believe this desired result.

That time came. Once more, the *septs* assembled, the mothers linked into the middle of the rings. Penetrations took place. Followed by the usual long, locked expectation.

Then ova issued.

How few! How disappointingly few ova!

Why were the mothers barren?

But the ova issuing, the progeny hatching in the air as before − were this time taking wing, hovering uncertainly over the multitude.

Conflicting cries of dismay and wonder filled the air. The noise alarmed the flying young. They set off towards the west on their new wings.

Despite the shouts of those below − their parents − to come back, to come down, the fliers flew on, slowly flapping their unprecedented wings, and disappeared from the sight of the Parrot Generation.

After an hour or two, the fliers of Generation Nine became tired and settled on the plain. They huddled close, rested unaccustomed muscles. There were no more than four hundred of them; they were oppressed by the solitude, the mute desolation of the place.

All round them lay the plain, covered in its mysterious patterns, leading nowhere. Deep silence prevailed.

At length, a venturesome *sept* struggled into the air

and spiralled higher and higher, in an attempt to see what lay beyond the plain. Up and up they climbed, until the ground was lost in haze. The air became sultry. Still they flew. Far, far above them, they glimpsed a pale globe, thrilling in its implications. Then their strength failed them, and they had to glide back to earth. They landed convinced that they had seen the sun at last. But of the plain there had been no visible end.

After more practice, the flying Generation Nine found itself able to stay aloft without fatigue. It continued in the direction the Tribe had maintained over the generations, making for the west, winging along close to the ground, stopping only to sleep or eat. So its days were passed, eternally on the wing.

Generation Ten numbered only thirty-two thousand, but at least numbers were increasing. Some of them were born without wings. These unfortunates were left behind without compunction. Generation Ten was sure of itself, and sure of reaching its destination, flying great distances without rest. Still the dull brownish landscape unrolled below, without feature or monument.

It was this generation, in its over-confidence, which almost came to grief. No longer did they bother to post sentries while they rested. The Enemy was nothing more than a fairy story, told to scare or amuse before they closed their eyes for sleep. The Twenty-One had passed beyond legend, becoming mistier than the horizon itself. Even their dreams were dreams of disbelief.

And then the Forager came.

The Forager was gigantic beyond imagining. Those waking to look upwards in incredulous horror could see only its fangs, lubricated and clicking in anticipation. With a body suspended high in the air. Great

124

To the Zambill fell the larger part of the mountain, stocked with small game and watered by brooks. The Antall, in the east, had their sacred pools in the rocks, and lived off the great variety of birds which nested among the crags of the broken hill.

In accord with these marginal variations in territory, the two tribes observed different customs. Their customs governed every event in life, from birth to death, including such matters as food, and how to cook and eat it.

Both tribes were patriarchal, and ruled by savage chiefs. When the young men reached puberty, they were forced to undergo initiation rites. These rites also differed between the tribes. The youths of the Antall were required to disappear into the wastes of the hill, there to slay a mountain cat barehanded. Before the youths of the Zambill could become fully-fledged warriors, they had to vanish into the rocks of the higher hill, there to mate with a female baboon.

The local game, needless to say, did not observe human customs. When chased, goat, cat and mountain sheep often fled to the heights, jumping across the gulf of King's Leap to safety from their pursuers. This frontier meant nothing to them. But one day, two old men met at King's Leap, and confronted each other across its rocky lips.

Of recent years, drought had stricken this part of the world, and game was scarce. The result was an intensification of the hostility between the Antall and the Zambill. Any member of the other tribe who was captured was put to death after cruel torture. Raids were undertaken, crops and huts burned, women raped, children taken into slavery.

The instigator of warlike activity on the Zambill side was Chief Whiili-An. On the western slopes of the broken hill stood a gate of clumsy design, its two round towers linked by a wooden gallery stretching

stalks of legs, angled this way and that, supported the body.

Unlike the steady monotonous movements of the Tribe, the Forager's movements were rapid but intermittent, a veritable stutter of muscles. A blurr of action, death of an individual, stillness – then fast swallowing as the warm food went down. Then stillness again, followed by another swift pounce.

Terrified, Generation Ten took to flight. It had no weapons of offence, no defence but retreat; but its anger and surprise was such that all its members swooped on new wings down into the eyes of the monstrous invader.

Those eyes, various and fur-rimmed, seemed to burn darkly for a moment – until spiked feet quenched them. Then the Forager reared like a startled horse, combing the air with its leading limbs. Then it ran blinded from its attackers.

Its high jointed legs carried it rapidly over the plain. It plunged away on an erratic course. Long after the thin limbs were lost in the haze, the bulbous body could still be seen, bobbing above the undulating ground.

Ten of the Tribe had been killed. The remainder, much disturbed by what had transpired, flew to a nearby strip of purple, there to rest and discuss what they should do.

A stale, sluggish wind blew across the face of the endless plain, carrying dust with it. The survivors of Generation Ten huddled close together. They had lost the initiative even to forage for Arntrods.

It was then, in this hour of despair, that one of the individuals chanced to look towards the northwest.

In excitement, he called to the others. Soon all were staring where he pointed. It seemed they could see something, they knew not what.

Together, they mounted into the air, climbing high, ever watching as they circled.

There was no doubt. A formation of some kind lay low to the north-west. The general opinion was that it was a range of mountains, half-concealed by the haze. There was to be an end to the plain at last.

Somewhere there must lie a land promised by the ancestors, where food was abundant, where there was shelter and variety of forms and a more pleasing way of life.

The Tribe landed again, abuzz with excitement.

And at that moment enormous lights lit the sky overhead, such as none had ever known. And there were huge roaring noises. The ground shook. And a dazzling brilliance such as they had never known shone down from above and extinguished them.

Consolations of Age

The hill was broken and, on the face of it, fo
Two tribes lived on the hill, the Antall or
slopes, and the Zambill on the west.

Perched in their watchtowers, the tribes
welcoming savannah and jungle. From the
those distant trees they had come, and to it tl
return, had not fiercer tribes driven ther
present refuge and taken over their ancestr
Their defeat, their flight, was not forgot
hunted with circumspection.

A stranger knowing something of the his
two tribes might suppose that they would
selves against common, powerful enemies.
so. The Antall and Zambill were perpetu.
with each other.

That they survived at all was due to an
geology. The broken hill was all that was l
had once been a great mountain, drained
river. Just as all that remained of the mount
hill, so all that remained of the river was a
rock, deep but fairly narrow, which divi\
into two unequal parts – the land of the Ar
land of the Zambill. This cleft was know\
Leap.

across the top of the doors. Behind this gate was the citadel of Zambill, a crowded, uncomfortable place which gave shelter to animals and insects as well as humans. The towers were of stone, the inhabitants were stony-faced, and behind the market square stood the stone palace of Chief Whiili-An. Here he lived with his five wives, plotting destruction on the enemies of his tribe. The skulls of past enemies, grinning from his walls, were constant reminders of his prowess.

Just as relentless was Chief Maani-Mjmu of the Antall. He lived with his six wives in a decorated mud fortress behind the mud walls of his citadel on the eastern slopes. His life was dedicated to inspiring his warriors to fresh atrocities against their neighbours on the other side of the hill. His fortress bore on its battlements gruesome testimony to his past successes.

Many a night, under the great moons that sailed over the hill, blood was drunk in the citadels of Antall and Zambill, and yet another victory of one or other chief was celebrated with drumbeat, sweat and liquor.

Within their own territories, the word of Chief Whiili-An and of Chief Maani-Mjmu was law, and unchallenged. Only one thing prevailed above their word. That was the custom of the tribe.

It so happened that in both tribes the chiefs were worshipped as gods. But when divinity fell from the brow of the god, a younger chief was appointed, who immediately despatched the old god without mercy or reference to his previously unblemished record. The tests for failing divinity differed between the tribes, although both were equally stringent.

One afternoon late in the year, when the sky was full of flocks of mourner-birds passing overhead for days at a time, Chief Maani-Mjmu of the Antall climbed to the top of the eastern side of the hill and stood leaning on his spear, breathing hard, and looking down into the abyss of King's Leap. While he rested there, an old man appeared on the western side of the Leap and slowly drew nearer.

Although Maani-Mjmu's eyesight was not what it had been, he knew this must be an enemy. He prepared to fight. Then he recognised Chief Whiili-An of the Zambill.

Chief Whiili-An saw the stationary figure at the same time and recognised his enemy. Hefting their spears, they confronted each other.

Both were bony and pot-bellied. Their eyes were sunken. Their skin was finely wrinkled, as if time had cast a specially tailored net over them.

For thirty years, they had been at war. To each, the other ranked as little less than a demon. So engrossed had they been in the organisation of hunting and fighting, that neither had noticed the years go by. But great suns had plunged into the Savannah, great moons had sailed above the jungles; sons had grown up and wives had grown old. Somewhere beneath the skin, below the bone, a magic spell of decay had been cast – a spell which finally even gods had been forced to recognise.

'You thief, you fecundator of monkeys!' shouted Maani-Mjmu. 'I piss in your food-bowl.'

'You murderer, you strangler of feline young!' called back Whiili-An. 'My dung shall daub your cheeks.'

Both men began to jump up and down, waving their spears and bawling ritual insults across the frontier.

Finally, Maani-Mjmu stopped and said, 'Phew, that's enough. I'll have to sit down.' He stooped and seated himself carefully on the edge of King's Leap.

Whiili-An hesitated, scratching his greying hair. Then he said, 'That's not a bad idea. My legs aren't what they were.'

They sat facing each other across the divide, listening to the stridulations of the cicadas.

130

Finally, Whiili-An said, 'Well, you old villain, I suppose they've decided you're no longer a god.'

Maani-Mjmu said nothing for a long while. His silence was adequate answer. 'How about you, you old brute?' he asked.

Whiili-An sighed. 'I may as well tell you, since it's plain you're now no better than a clapped-out old cormorant. I'm up here for my divinity test. I've got to jump across this stupid King's Leap. I know I'll never do it. It's too wide for anyone to jump. Only a fool would try.'

'I hear you tried and managed it last year,' said Maani-Mjmu maliciously.

'My left leg's been playing me up lately, to tell the truth,' Whiili-An said. 'Anyhow, smartass, what are you up here for?'

Maani-Mjmu let another of his long silences elapse.

'Never mind having to jump over this ridiculous abyss,' he said. 'I've got to jump *into* it. I've just failed my divinity test.'

His enemy eyed him craftily. 'Which was?'

'You know.'

'How should I know the customs of a gang of poachers?'

'Well, I failed to satisfy all my six wives when we performed before the warriors last night.' Maani-Mjmu hung his head.

Whiili-An laughed again, slapping his knees.

Growing angry, Maani-Mjmu got to his feet and brandished his spear.

'You gibbering gorilla, I satisfied five of them before daybreak.'

'You couldn't satisfy a female dog turd.'

'I'll satisfy you, you python fart!' So saying, Maani-Mjmu flung his spear. It missed his enemy by a hand's breadth, as once it would never have done, and skittered harmlessly across bare rock.

Scared, Whiili-An hurled his weapon, only to miss the other old chief by a few inches.

'They don't make spears the way they used to', he said, scratching his thigh.

'Well, the damned women don't cook like they used to,' Maani-Mjmu explained. 'You see, if the women won't cook properly, the men don't make spears properly. I've told them dozens of times. Do you think they listen?'

'You've nothing to complain about. You should see the trouble we have in Zambill. The warriors are lazy. They sit on their bums all day. No wonder the women won't cook for them.'

'With us, it's the other way round. The women won't cook properly so the men won't work properly.'

'So you just said, you old nut. Are you going cracked in your old age?'

'Cracked or not, I could jump this leap, which is more than you can do.'

'You could never jump that,' Whiili-An said, spitting into the gulf to show his contempt.

'I could have done last year.'

'Do it now.'

'Tomorrow. My back's troubling me a bit today.'

The sun prepared to plunge into the savannah, wreathing itself with band after band of purple heat.

'It's a silly test, anyhow,' Whiili-An said, turning away. 'I always said it's a silly test. Doesn't prove a thing about a man's ability. This last year or so I tried to get the custom changed, but your warrior of today is a bone-headed fellow. Won't listen. Refuses to listen.'

'Don't talk to me about the younger generation. When I think of all the things I've done for them . . . ' His voice trailed off into bitterness.

'Maybe we could join forces, you and I, and start a new tribe,' Whiili-An said, as the sun disappeared.

'What was it *like*,' Maani-Mjmu asked, as the moon

appeared. 'You know, mating with that female baboon?'

Whiili-An laughed. He settled himself more comfortably on his side of the abyss. 'Funny you should ask that. I was thinking about it only the other night. You see, the trick is to drop on the animal from above . . . ' He laughed again. 'Well, I might as well tell you the whole story. We've got plenty of time . . . '

The O in José

They had seen no human habitation for two days
when they came unexpectedly on a mountain village.
Here their servant arranged that an old woman should
guide them over the mountains and back to civili-
sation.

After spending an uncomfortable night in the
village, they were off early next morning, the five of
them: the old woman on foot, the servant on a mule
leading a pack mule, and the three men on horses. Of
the men, one was by some years the oldest, a spare
man with a trim white beard and somewhat over-
meticulous gestures. The two younger men were of
contrasting type; one of them, the *bon viveur*, was a
thick-set man in his forties, with a plump face and an
intelligent glance not entirely marred by a snub nose.
His humorous manner acted as a foil for the more
serious ways of the youngest man, who was a philatelist of some repute, although only among other phil-
atelists.

Each of the men was pleased with the excellent
company afforded by his two fellows. They had established among themselves a combination of serious-
ness and gaiety, of reserve and intimacy, which is rare
and which more than compensated for the ardours of

their long and difficult journey. Where the road would allow it, they spent much of each morning, before the sun was too hot, conversing as they rode; and these conversations were often protracted after dusk, while the servant prepared and they ate their supper.

But now, as the old woman led them higher into the hills, and as the scene became more desolate, the elder fell silent. The *bon viveur* was delivering a long mock-heroic about why people told stories of what their dentists did, but finally he too lapsed into silence. All that morning, they rode in a quiet broken only by the echoes of the horses' movements among the canyons they traversed, or by an occasional word from the servant to his mules.

The *bon viveur* secretly resented this silence that he felt radiated from the elder and rebuked him inwardly for not thrusting off a fit of old man's melancholy. His feeling was that they were three intelligent men whose inward resources should be proof against transitory outside influences. So when they stopped at midday to take the cold meat, wine, and coffee that the servant set before them, the *bon viveur* said to the philatelist in a provoking tone, 'Our old guide woman is more silent and dismal even than we are. We've not had a word out of her, or out of us.'

'She has more right to be taciturn than we have,' the philatelist said with a laugh. 'Think what awaits us over the mountains: hot baths, music, elevators to whisk us to choice restaurants, libraries, conversation, the company of fair women! What awaits her? Only that dreadful village again, and work till her life's end.' Addressing himself to the old woman in her own tongue, he called, 'Hey, my charming madam, you only left your home at dawn today! Are you pining already for some vagabond of a husband?'

The old woman had come barefoot from the village with seemingly no provision for the three- or four-day journey but a loaf tucked under her shawl. She sat now away from them, awaiting the order to move on again, and did not look up or answer when the philatelist spoke.

'You'll have to find something else to distract yourself with,' the elder said, not approving this baiting of an old woman.

As they got up to go, and were mounting their horses, the servant came over and told the *bon viveur* and the philatelist, rather shame-facedly, that he had heard in the village that the old woman was once a great beauty who had suffered a great love and a great betrayal.

The *bon viveur* laughed and nudged his friend in the ribs. 'All these old crones claim to have been great beauties,' he said. 'We shall indeed have to find something else to distract ourselves with.'

Although the elder smarted a little at this remark, which he felt to be directed against him, he said nothing, and they rode on; but as it happened it was only a half hour later that they found something to distract them back into their old companionable humour.

They worked their way through a defile, the end of which was marked by one wretched tree clinging to the rockface, and were suddenly on a plateau. To one side lay mountain peaks, ribbed with snow and half-hidden under fuming cloud, while to the other lay an immense panorama of the land they had so painfully traversed, all the way to the distant sea, now hidden in the hazes of noon. With a common instinct, the three men turned aside from the way the woman led and directed their mounts toward the precipice.

For a long while they stood drinking in this view of the distant world of grass and shade and fertility, so different from the place in which they now stood. At last the elder said, 'Well, I still say there is nothing more melancholy than a mountain, but it was worth the journey just to look down at this spectacle. Sometime, I would like to have you gentlemen's opinions on why a view from a height has such power to move the spirit.'

'Come and look at this!' exclaimed the philatelist. Something in his voice made the others turn immediately to see what he had found.

Perched a few feet away from them, on the very lip of the plateau, so that its outer edge hung into space, was a giant rock. It was grey in colour, and most of its surface had been worn smooth by the elements. But what drew the attention of the men was a human addition to the rock. Someone had carved here in its centre, and in large letters, the name JOSÉ.

'Well, that's a disappointment, I must say,' the *bon viveur* remarked humorously. 'Just when I was thinking we were the first people ever to set foot in this remote spot.'

'I wonder who José was, and why he carved his name here of all places,' the elder said. 'And when. And a dozen other questions connected with the mysterious José.'

'Perhaps he carved this as his memorial and then jumped over the edge,' suggested the *bon viveur*. 'I can think of few more dramatic spots in which to commit suicide, if one were so inclined.'

'I've an idea,' said the philatelist. 'Here we have a little mystery at our very feet. Let's each tell a story about this José. Obviously, it is beyond our power to arrive at the truth about him, so let's each arrive at a fiction about him.'

'Good idea,' said the *bon viveur*, 'though I have run out of bright ideas. The oldest among us must tell his José story first.'

'Seconded,' agreed the philatelist and, turning to the elder man, asked him to think of a story.

The elder stroked his beard a little and protested that he was being given the hardest task in beginning; but he was a resourceful old man and, setting one foot on the carved rock, he stared into space and began his story.

'I am not at all sure,' he said, 'that this name was not written here by supernatural means, for this plainly is a supernatural place. If I have doubts, it is because José is hardly a supernatural name. Of all names it is the most earthy; all round the world, you can find peasants called José or Joe or Jozé or some close local equivalent. Of all names, it is the most impersonal, the name of a force rather than a man. You know, in the first human tribe, all the males were probably called José.

'Consider the letters that form the name. Look at this three-fingered É! It reminds one, doesn't it, of a crude agricultural implement, a rake that every peasant uses to rake the detritus of each season wearily from his land. And the J! Isn't that another implement, the first, the curving sickle that must cut down the weeds and the choking grass from the land? What about this awkward S he has made in the rock, of all the letters the most difficult to cut? Is it not the slow meandering path taken by his beast, along the shores of a lake, or winding over a mountain track? And look at the O in JOSÉ! What a symbol you have there, my friends – a symbol of the earth itself, which José will inherit, and of fertility, which is as much the concern of the Josés of our world as it is of the earthworm. You see what José means; it is a natural force like the rock on which it is written.

'But this particular inscription has something individual about it, I fancy. You notice how the J is bitten deep, but the other letters are formed more shallowly. The E is too small. It all goes to show that this José lacked assurance. You may wonder why, and I will tell you.

'This José was a quiet boy, not particularly clever, not particularly dull, not particularly brave, not particularly anything. But one day when he was going on the way to his father's house, he was stopped in the lane by four bigger boys. José did not know these boys, and we can imagine that directly he saw them he could tell from their looks that there was trouble coming. Perhaps he tried to run from them, but they caught him and made him stand before them.

' "What is your name?" they demanded.

' "José."

' "OK, José – explain yourself."

'He tried to evade the question, indeed he tried to evade them, but always they grabbed him by the collar and said "Explain yourself."

' "I was born in the village," he said pathetically at last.

' "Why were you born, boy? Explain yourself."

'No answer he could give seemed to satisfy them. Moreover, the answers were not satisfactory even to José himself. When finally he escaped, their question worried him even more than his fresh bruises. Explain himself? He was totally unable to do so! Now it would be foolish of me to claim, even as an omniscient storyteller with the power of life and death over my character, that José never forgot that searching demand to explain himself. But let us say that it would come back to him at odd and sometimes inconvenient moments in his life, to puzzle and worry him: when he was making merry with his friends, when he was flirting with a village girl, or perhaps when one of them jilted him; or when he was in church, or ill, or taking a holiday, or swimming in the river, or lying lazily in his marriage bed, or cradling his firstborn, or sweating in the noonday field, or even squatting in the flimsy W.C. at the bottom of his patch of land. What I mean to say is, that at various moments throughout

José's life, the good ones or the bad, he would suddenly feel that a big question hung over him, that there was something about him that needed explaining, something that he was quite unable to explain.

'He kept this thing secret, even from his wife whom he loved. He told himself it was not important, and you two gentlemen may like to judge if he was correct in so thinking. But not to let my story grow too long, for I grant you that stories about simple peasants can become very long indeed, José's wife died one day. He was full of grief, so much so that he persuaded his old mother to look after his son for a week while he himself saddled up the donkey and rode off into the hills to be alone with his melancholy. It's not my job to tell you why people have such an instinct, for to me hills are melancholy places in their own right, and more likely to induce than cure gloom. Still, for the purpose of my story, we have to have José riding into the hills – these hills, you know. The assumption will stand since it is not contrary to human nature.

'In the hills, José let the mule – no, we said donkey, didn't we? – he let the animal go where it would while he thought about his life and the meaning of life. But when it came to the meaning of life, he could no more explain himself than when he was a lad being bullied in the lane. In the depths of his brooding, he sat where we stand now, and he carved his name in this rock. And we three are not privileged to know whether José had the wit to see his name was his explanation, and that he himself was self-explanatory.'

This story was much appreciated by the *bon viveur* and the philatelist.

'I shall make a poor showing after that fine and philosophical story unless I have a drop of wine first,' said the *bon viveur*. He motioned to the servant, who now stood respectfully behind them, holding the horses. The old guide woman remained beyond the group, dissociating herself from them. When the servant came forward with a bag of wine and the *bon viveur* had slaked his throat, he said apologetically, 'Well, here is my story of José, though I'm afraid I'm going to have to move this hulking boulder over to another site for the purposes of the narrative.'

'It is the privilege of fiction to move mountains,' observed the philatelist, and with that encouragement, the *bon viveur* began his tale.

'With a certain amount of diligence, it was possible to grow very good vines in José's field. His field lay at the foot of a mountain next to a lake, so that it was sheltered and it was not too arduous to get water to moisten the roots of the vines.

'José was cross-eyed. He had other and more serious troubles also. The field was small, and would barely support him and his pigs and his donkey. Then there were the changes of government, and the changes of forms of government; and although each form of government proclaimed itself more interested in José's welfare than the last, each one seemed to require José to work harder than the last.

'There was also the rock. The rock was shaped like an elephant's foot and had fallen away from the mountain in some forgotten time, perhaps even before there were men to forget, or indeed elephants to have feet. The rock occupied a lot of José's land where he might more profitably have grown vines. But he never resented it. On his twenty-first birthday he carved his name on it, and every day of his working life he rested his back against it.

'For all his troubles, José married a good girl from the nearby town and was happy with her. She possessed the sound sense to love him for his crossed eye and to smell sweet even when she sweated from labouring in the field with him. He planted his vines closer to the mountain and worked harder than

142

before, in order to support her and the government.

'A son was born to José. José rejoiced, and planted his vines closer to the lake. A second son was born, and the vines were planted closer to the big rock. In due season, the next year to be precise, a third son was born. After the rejoicing was done, José planted his vines closer together. And he worked a little harder, and got a little drunk when he thought he worked too hard.

'The years came and went as fast as governments, and the sons grew up tall and scraggy because there was not overmuch to eat. The eldest son drifted into town and became full of the theories of the current régime. He came back to see his father wearing a steel-grey suit and said: "Father, you are a reactionary and obtuse old fool of a goat, if you will pardon my saying so. If you let the government buy your land for a reasonable pittance, you could go on working on it and they would come with dynamite and blast that elephant's foot out of the way, so that you could grow many more vines than you do – increase production, as we call it in the city." He even got a man to photograph the rock with a foreign-made camera, but José was not to be moved.

The government fell, and the first son was shot for his ideas. The second son joined the army. One day, he came back to see his father dressed in a captain's uniform and said, 'So, Dad, you antiquated old numbskull, I see you are still toiling your life out round the elephant's foot! Did you never learn what graft was when you were young? The army are going to build a new road a couple of kilometres from here. Give me the word and I'll send them the rock to build the road with, and they can haul it away with bull-dozers." He even got a sergeant to survey and photograph the rock, but José was no more to be moved than his rock.

143

'There was a revolution, and the second son was shot for the good of the country. The youngest son grew up very crafty, perhaps because he had starved the most, and went into banking. He saw what little effect his brothers' words had had on his father, and addressed the old man thus, "My dear and hard-working old paternal pop, my informed friends in the city tell me there is every reason to suspect that there may be a great well of oil under the elephant's foot. You could be rich beyond the dreams of avarice and buy mother two new frocks if that were so. Why do you not look? If you and mother broke down a barrow-load of rock each day and flung it into the lake, at the end of two years or maybe less or maybe more, you would have the land clear. I can get you a barrow wholesale if you agree." He even induced a fellow banker to take a colour photograph of the rock, but José was not to be moved.

'The next day, the president of the country absconded with all the gold from the bank, and the government fell. But José's wife sent the three photographs of the rock that looked so like an elephant's foot to a big magazine, whereupon it became a great tourist attraction at twenty-five cents a time, and José never had to grow vines any more.'

The elder and the philatelist greatly enjoyed this story, the latter especially since he was by profession a banker and appreciated the dig his friend had had at him.

'So I must now tell my José story,' he said, 'which I certainly shall not enjoy as much as yours. To ensure that it has at least some merit I will borrow elements from both your tales, the peasant and the rock. But if you don't mind we will leave such trivial items as bankers and revolutions out of it and look at the whole matter in its proper perspective.'

So saying, he embarked upon his story.

'Imagine a sheet of ice, miles and miles wide, covering much of the world. At its most extensive, it reached only half way up the mountain. Then it grew grey, and crumpled and melted and disappeared. In its place, a lake formed, lying at the foot of the mountain.

'Slowly the weather grew warmer. It became hot by day, though the nights remained cool. Several times, the mountain split and its flanks fell into the lake. Things grew on these piles of stones, and along the new ground exposed by the lake as it shrank. In spring, the whole shelf was covered with yellow flowers.

'Distantly, a river broke through on a new course and poured its waters into the lake, whereupon the lake stopped shrinking. Things swam in the lake; some of them climbed out of the lake. Some of those that climbed out died in the field, but others gained new qualities and flourished.

'One of the animals was ungainly and slow. In the palm of its skull lay a pool of mud through which trickled the waters of its new discovery called thought. It sank into the rock. Of its thought there remained no trace, but the pattern of its bones lay in the quiet strata, making a blueprint more pleasing than in life.

'Another animal was full of a vast and automatic fury. Its cry when it hunted cut like a knife and struck the rocks with the force of a hammer. One day, a slab of the mountainside fell upon it, and the slab resembled the head of a serpent.

'Another creature was patient. It tilled the soil between the mountain and the lake and planted vines in the soil and tended them year by year. When it was young, it carved its name JOSÉ on the rock shaped like a serpent head, and spent the rest of its life in the field, working everywhere round the rock. One day it staggered into the shade of the rock and never rose again.

145

'Another being learned to extract the energy it required direct from the soil. It bloomed and ferreted and crackled, and again part of the mountain fell, making an avalanche that splashed into the lake for half a day. The thing slowly annihilated the rubble from the mountain, until it disintegrated from ripeness.

'Now a being of splendour arose which could extract its necessary energy from the whole universe, and so needed to pay no attention to mountain, field, or lake. Because it was sufficient to itself, it destroyed all other life and sat through an eternity sketching elaborate patterns of light in its being, until it was itself translated into light.

'The last thing was a thing of infinite love and infinite might. It grieved for the destruction that had been and determined to create a new system of life based only remotely on the old. It looked about at the silent mountain and lake; finally it built an entire new universe, shaping it out of the O in JOSÉ that was carved in the serpent head rock.

'On planets in the new universe, mountains and lakes began to appear. They worked out their own enormous processes in solitude, for the being of love and might had built them a universe safe from life.'

The *bon viveur* and the elder both declared themselves impressed by this story, and the latter added, 'You take a more bleak and long view of humanity than I dare to at my time of life. You don't really find life as meaningless as all that, do you?'

The philatelist spread his hands. 'Yes, sometimes I do – in a place like this, for instance. We are only passing through, and our mood will change. But look at the wretched old guide woman, for instance. What has life to offer her? And look at the region in which she lives, at this profound and aloof grandeur all about us. Is not its meaning greater and more enduring than man's?'

146

The elder shuddered. 'My friend, I prefer to believe that this mountain has no meaning at all until it is translated through man's understanding.'

As he spoke, the servant touched him respectfully on the arm. 'Excuse me, sir, but I think we really ought to be moving on, because we don't want to be still up here in this exposed place when night falls.'

'You are absolutely right, my friend. You are a practical man. All our endeavours should be devoted towards getting away from this lifeless tomb. Whoever José was, he has no interest for any of us now. Tell the old woman to lead on.'

They mounted their horses and turned away from the rock with its brief inscription. They followed the servant across the drab and stony soil. The old woman led them on, never once casting her eye back at the spot where, as a young and passionate woman, she had blazed the name of her faithless lover.

A Romance of the Equator

Friends, very long ago in the old tropical green world, a boy lived whose name was Kahlin. Two strange things befell him in his life.

First of all, when he was a mere youth, with limbs smooth as twigs, his home was demolished by a volcanic eruption. So great was that explosion that it could be heard by man and beast all round the world. Pieces of the earth were thrown into the air and landed across the seas two hundred miles and more away, where they still stand today as lines of hills.

The volcano destroyed Kahlin's home and killed both his parents and his little brothers.

Kahlin was so frightened that he ran and ran towards the north, away from the eruption. His legs carried him eventually to a narrow isthmus, fringed on either side by cliffs which fell sheer to the sea.

The boy heard a pathetic crying. He went to the edge of the nearest cliff and looked down. Two young gazelles had fallen over the side and were resting perilously on a ledge some feet below. Every effort they made to scramble up again endangered their foothold on the ledge. He could see that they were doomed to slip and fall.

Being a compassionate boy, Kahlin removed his

149

cloth headgear and used it as a rope to lower himself to the gazelles. He took one of the poor little things under each arm and climbed with them up to safety.

The animals were exhausted. He improvised shelter for them that night on the far side of the isthmus, and lay down between them, gazing piteously into their faces. One of the gazelles was white, the other brown. He put his arms about them and slept.

During the warmth of the night he heard a sound like the distant booming of the sea. He woke at dawn, and found that the two gazelles had turned into young women. They lay naked beside him, their eyes closed, one brown, one white. Still he held them, and his heart beat strongly and his breath came fast as he gazed at their beauty.

The two girls awoke and gazed at him, the white one with blue eyes, the brown one with eyes of amber.

Kahlin had heard of such things happening in fairy tales, so he covered his nudity and said to the girls, 'How beautiful you are, both of you! My guess is that you were both princesses, turned into animals by some great enchanter. Is that so?'

The girls sat up and concealed some of their nudity. They denied that what Kahlin said was true. 'We were animals, and were happy as animals. It is only the enchantments of your love which make you see us as girls. You are in a spell, not us.'

'So how do you see me?' he asked.

'As a handsome male gazelle.'

He snorted with disappointment, but the girls said sweetly, 'We love you as we see you, and you must be content to be loved according to our interpretation. Truly, if we saw you as you see yourself, we could not love you.'

Because he was a sensible boy, Kahlin saw some force in this argument and, because the world was young and its core still molten, he made love to the

150

two girls, to the brown and the white, with equal passion.

Afterwards, the girls rose up and bathed themselves in the sea for a long while, standing below a waterfall, and washing each other's hair, the fair hair and the black. They wove themselves grass skirts before returning to Kahlin's side.

They regarded him with their large gazelle eyes and said, 'Now the time is come when you must choose between us. It is not right that you should have us both. You must choose me or my sister to be yours, and to accompany you through the world until the last sunset, whilst the rejected sister goes on her way.'

Kahlin grew angry and swore that he could not choose between them. They insisted. He threw himself down on the grass in a passion, beating the earth, swearing he loved them both, the one with hair like a raven's wing, and the one with hair like honey.

'But we are going to live in different parts of the world,' one sister said. 'The pale to the north, the dark to the south.'

Still he swore that he loved them both equally and would die if either left him. Dusk fell and they were still arguing.

A moon rose like a washed shell on the blue beaches of the sky, and eventually the girls came to an agreement. They said to Kahlin, 'We see that you hold us both dear. Very well, since you saved us both from death on the cliff, then we will make a bargain with you. You shall enjoy us both, but a price must be paid, and that price must be your peace of mind. You will be forever trying to decide which of us you love the better, the brown or the white.'

'I shall love you both the same.'

Both girls shook their heads wisely, and wagged admonitory fingers, white and brown.

'But that is impossible. Since we are different, so we

must be loved differently. Did you not know that this is one of the great secret truths of human companionship, and the cause of all its torment as well as its happiness? There is a configuration of love to fit the needs of every configuration of personality.'

He threw his arms round them, crying, 'There's no difference between you, except that one of you is brown and one white. How can I ever say which I love best, the limbs of ivory or the limbs of gold?'

And the two girls smiled first at him and then at each other, saying, 'Just as you see us only as female, so your love makes you blind to our real differences, which are many. But you will grow to see. Your blindness will not long protect you.'

'You women talk too much,' Kahlin said, clapping his hands together. 'I will accept the terms of your bargain and love you both.' Whereupon, he coaxed them to lie down beside him, and the women did not take a lot of coaxing.

The moon set. It rose and set again many times, undergoing its small but magical span of changes, rather like a chime blown by the wind. And with every moon, Kahlin grew older in experience.

He saw that it was as the girls said. They differed greatly in their natures. He could scarcely believe it. In the first flush of his love, he had been blind to their personalities.

Then they had seemed merely like personages from some deep dream. Now they slowly became human, with all their faults and contradictions.

One of the women was extremely passionate, and desired always to be close to Kahlin, never letting him from her sight. The other woman was cooler and more casual in her manner, teasing him in a way that alternately infuriated and delighted him.

One of the women was a good cook, and spent long hours over her stove, preparing with infinite patience dishes of great delicacy which could scarcely appease the appetite. The other woman cooked indifferently, yet bestirred herself occasionally to provide a great feast which they ate till their stomachs groaned.

One of the women was not greatly fond of washing, and was lazy, and spent much of her time lying about with her toes curled, prattling and laughing. The other woman was as neat and clean as a cat, and spent her days trying to keep everything impossibly tidy.

One of the women was highly intelligent, making clever or amusing remarks, and scolding Kahlin for his ignorance. The other woman was not intelligent, and repeated everything Kahlin said in honest admiration for his cleverness.

One of the women was most active by day, and leaped up with the dawn, calling Kahlin and her sister to join her. The other woman was a night creature, and came alive only after sunset, when she seemed to glow with a special light.

One woman was frank in all things, the other rather dishonest, full of amazing little secrets.

One woman painted and decorated herself, the other refused to do anything of the sort.

One woman had a gift for music and danced beautifully, the other could not sing a note but designed exquisite clothes for the three of them.

One woman smelt of musk, the other of honeysuckle.

One woman liked to talk about forbidden things, and cast a languishing eye on other men, while the other made a mystery of herself and disliked Kahlin's men friends.

One woman kept a pet monkey that pulled Kahlin's ears, while the other doted on three cats.

One woman seemed to be never quite content, whilst the other was completely uncritical.

One woman let her hair grow long, while the other cut hers short.

As the years went by, one woman became surprisingly plump, while the other became surprisingly thin.

By the same token, Kahlin also grew old, and his hair turned grey. No longer was his step as certain as it had been, or his gaze so keen.

Every day of his life he worked for the two women, and felt his love split between the brown and the white. Finally he rose and said to them, 'Although I still have strength, yet I now know my days to be numbered. I have a desire to return to my origins, so I am going back to the mountains where I lived with my parents before the volcano erupted. You may come with me, or you may stay here, as you please.'

This was in part his way of testing them, for he thought that perhaps only one – the white or the brown woman – would follow him on his journey.

So he travelled without looking back. He could hear that someone walked behind him, yet he refused to allow himself to turn to see who it was. He crossed over the isthmus where he had saved the two gazelles, the brown and the white, so many years ago that he went past the spot before recalling it.

Still he plodded on, and came at last to the mountains where he had been born. As he climbed the sides of the final hill, scenes from the distant past swam before his eyes. Recollecting his parents with love, he was granted insight, and perceived for the first time how his father and mother had differed in every way, almost as his two women differed. Only his childish love, with its quality of blindness, had allowed him to see his parents as two equal gods.

'So I glean a grain of knowledge,' he said aloud to himself. 'Was it worth travelling all these years for?' But he answered himself that a grain of insight was indeed better than nothing.

peered over the lip of the great crater to disperse its dews, they rose and launched their boat towards the island.

The two women stood by him with their arms entwined about his shoulders, and teased him, saying, 'So, after all these years, despite all your lack of peace of mind, you still cannot decide which of us you love the better, the one with the hair like honey or the one with hair like a raven's wing. Really, Kahlin, you are a funny man! Now you're stuck with us both for the rest of your life.'

The mysterious island was drifting nearer now. Kahlin could not help smiling, though he fixed his gaze upon the distant trees leaning out across the hazy waters, rather than on the two tormenting ladies by his side.

For he had his secret. Whereas once, as a youth, he had loved them because he thought they were almost identical, he had learnt through many long years to love them both more deeply because of their differences.